LEARNING
TO TALK TO
PLANTS

LEARNING TO TALK TO PLANTS

MARTA ORRIOLS

Translated from the Catalan
by Mara Faye Lethem

pushkin press

Pushkin Press
71–75 Shelton Street
London WC2H 9JQ

Learning to Talk to Plants was first published as *Aprendre a parlar amb les plantes* in
Barcelona, 2018

First published by Pushkin Press in 2020

The translation of this work has been supported by the Institut Ramon Llull

LLLL **institut
ramon llull**
Catalan Language and Culture

3 5 7 9 8 6 4 2

ISBN 13: 978-1-78227-577-0

Designed and typeset by Tetragon, London
Printed and bound by CPI Group (UK) Ltd, Croydon, CRO 4YY

www.pushkinpress.com

For you, Miquel.
Days and nights and those hours that can't be measured on a clock.
We'll never forget you.
I miss you and I love you. Still and forever.

"You put together two people who have not been put together before. Sometimes it is like that first attempt to harness a hydrogen balloon to a fire balloon: do you prefer crash and burn, or burn and crash? But sometimes it works, and something new is made, and the world is changed. Then, at some point, sooner or later, for this reason or that, one of them is taken away. And what is taken away is greater than the sum of what was there. This may not be mathematically possible; but it is emotionally possible."

JULIAN BARNES, *Levels of Life*

BEFORE

We were alive.

Terrorist attacks, accidents, wars and epidemics weren't our concern. We could watch movies that made light of dying, others that turned the act of dying into an act of love, but we remained outside that zone where the true meaning of death resided.

Some nights, protected by the arrogance of our late youth, we would lie in bed, surrounded by huge, soft pillows, and we would watch the news in the dim light, our feet intertwined, and that was when death, without us knowing, settled, all bluish, into the lenses of Mauro's glasses. One hundred and thirty-seven people died in Paris in attacks claimed by the Islamic State, six deaths in less than twenty-four hours on the roads in three different head-on collisions, an overflowing river caused four deaths in a small town in southern Spain, at least seventy dead in a chain of attacks in Syria. And, scared for a moment, we might have said things like "What a world" or "Poor guy, in the wrong place at the wrong time" and the news, if it wasn't too harsh, would dwindle that very night in the confines of the bedroom of a couple, a couple that was also fizzling out.

We would change the channel and watch the end of a movie, and meanwhile I'd confirm his arrival time the next day or remind him to go past the dry cleaner's to pick up his black coat; if we'd had a good day, in those last months, we might make love, but matter-of-factly. If the news was momentous, its effects would last a little longer, be part of the conversation on a coffee break at work or in line at the fishmonger's.

But we were alive, death was for others.

We used expressions like *I'm dead* to convey our exhaustion after a long day at work, and the word didn't affect our mood. When we were first together, we were capable of floating out in the middle of the sea at our favourite cove, and joking, with our lips drenched in salt and sun, about a hypothetical drowning that ended with a scandalous mouth-to-mouth scenario and cackles of laughter. Death was something distant, as if it didn't belong to us.

What I'd lived through as a girl—my mother became ill and died just a few months later—had become a hazy memory that no longer stung. My father came to pick me up at school just an hour after we'd come back from lunch. Hundreds of us, girls and boys, were climbing the spiral staircase to return to the classrooms from the cafeteria, with the high jinks typical of life, which keeps on moving despite the silence of those who are no longer among us. My father came to the classroom with the headmistress, who knocked on the door just as the science teacher was explaining that there were invertebrate animals and vertebrates. My memory of my mother's death will always be linked to white writing on the green chalkboard that divided the animal kingdom in two. My classmates, who up until then had always been

10

my equals, now looked at me with new eyes. I remained very still, overcome by the feeling that I was retreating to a third kingdom, the kingdom of wounded, motherless animals.

Even though it didn't make it any less terrible, that death was forewarned, and the warning had given us some time for goodbyes and well wishes, her decline gave us the chance to express all our love. Most of all, there was the naivety of believing she was going to the heaven that had been drawn for me, and the innocence of being seven years old, which saved me from comprehending the finality of her departure.

Mauro and I were a couple for many years. Then, and just for a few hours, we stopped being one. He died suddenly some months ago, without warning. The car that struck him carried him off, along with many other things.

Without the comfort of a heaven, and with all the unwieldy pain of adulthood, I often think and speak of Mauro using the adverbs *before* and *after*, to avoid the past tense. Life split down the middle. He was alive that afternoon with me, he drank wine and asked if they could cook his steak a bit more, he took a couple of calls from the publishing house while he played with his napkin ring, he jotted down, on the back of a business card from the restaurant, the title of a book by a French author he was enthusiastically recommending to me, he scratched his left earlobe, uncomfortable and ashamed, perhaps, and then he told me. He was almost stuttering. A few hours later he was dead.

The restaurant had a piece of coral in its logo. I look at it often, on that little card where Mauro, in his flawless handwriting, had written out that book title. Perhaps because we are all free to embellish our misfortune with as many fuchsias, yellows, blues and greens as our little hearts desire, since the day of the accident I imagine the before and after in my life like the Great Barrier Reef, the largest coral reef in the world. Every time I think about whether something happened before or after Mauro's death I make an effort to envisage the barrier reef, fill it with colourful fish and sea urchins, and turn it into an equator of life.

When death ceases to belong to others, you have to carefully make a place for it on the other side of the reef, because, otherwise, it feels completely within its rights to take up any and all available space.

Dying isn't mystical. Dying is physical, it's logical, it's real.

1

"Pili, check the equipment, fast! Is she breathing?"

"No."

"Let's start positive-pressure ventilation."

I repeat the baby's vitals in a whisper, like a litany. *I know, little one. This is no way to greet you on your arrival into this world, but we have to get you breathing, you hear me?*

"Thirty seconds." *One, two, three… there's a woman lying over there, your mum, and she needs you, you see her? Come on, you can do it, ten, eleven, twelve, thirteen… come on, breathe, you got this, I promise that if you can do this, things'll change, this world is a good place to be. Seventeen, eighteen, nineteen, twenty. Living is worth the effort, you know? Twenty-three, twenty-four… sometimes it's hard, I won't lie, twenty-six, twenty-seven, come on, sweetie, don't do this to me. I promise it's worth it. Thirty.*

Silence. The baby girl doesn't move.

"Pili, heart rate?"

My eyes meet the nurse's vigilant gaze. This is the second time this has happened recently and I know that warning look. She's right, I shouldn't raise my voice so much, I shouldn't raise it at all, in fact. I'm not comfortable. I'm hot and my right clog is rubbing against a little blister I got from my sandals in the last few days of my summer holiday. In these crucial moments, right after birth, the blister and

13

this heat are the last thing I need. Our absolute priority for the baby is to keep her from losing body warmth. Perhaps it wasn't such a good idea to travel at the crack of dawn and go straight to work without stopping by the house to unpack and shake off the strange sensation of having spent almost two weeks away, far from work, from my babies' medical records, from the blood work, from the lab, far from everything that makes me tick.

New decision. With short, quick movements, I stimulate the soles of the baby's feet and, as always happens when I do that, I curb my desire to press harder, with more urgency. *You can't do this to me, little one, I can't start September off like this, come on, breathe, pretty girl.* Reassessment.

I try to concentrate on the information on the monitor and on the girl, but I need to close my eyes for a second since I can't cover my ears, and the questions launched at me by her mother, which sound like a disconsolate moan in the delivery room, throw me off worse than ever. Other people's suffering now feels like an overloaded plate after I've eaten my fill. I can't take in any more and it sends me running in the opposite direction. Every pained cry and whimper becomes Mauro's mother's sobbing on the day of his burial. It ripped at the soul.

Breathe, pretty girl, come on, for the love of God, breathe!

I furrow my brow and shake my head to remind myself that I shouldn't stir up all that. Not here. Here you shouldn't make waves. Here you shouldn't remember. Not here, Paula. Focus. Reality hits me like a pitcher of cold water and instantly puts me in my place: I have a body weighing only eight hundred and fifty grams that hasn't taken a breath, laid out here on the resuscitation table, and its life is in my hands. My sixth sense kicks in, guiding me more and more. That sense somehow maintains a balance between the most extreme objectivity, where I retain protocols and reasoning, and my shrewd ability to harness my intuition, without which, I'm convinced, I couldn't aid these tiny creatures with their arrival into the world.

Listen, little girl, one of the things worth living for is the sea.

"Pili, I'm turning off the ventilation. I'm going to try tactile stimulation of her back."

I take a deep breath and let it out like someone preparing to leap into the void. My mask acts as a wall and holds in my exhalation, a mix of the fluoride toothpaste I found this morning in my father's bathroom and the quick, bitter coffee I drank in a motorway service station. I miss my things, my normal life. I miss my coffee and my coffeemaker. The smell of home, my rhythm, not owing anyone any explanations, just being able to do my own thing.

I rub the baby's tiny back as gently as I can.

The sea has a rhythm, you feel it? Like this: it comes and it goes, it comes and it goes. You feel my hands? The waves come and go, like this. Come on, beauty, the sea is worth living for, there are other things too, but for now focus on the sea, like this, gentle, you feel it?

"She's breathing."

The first cry was like a miaow, but we received it with the joyful relief that greets a summer storm.

"Welcome…" I'm not sure if I'm saying it to the baby or to myself, but I have to struggle to hold back my emotion.

I wash her with quick movements I've made hundreds of times before. It calms me to see her colour improving, that transparent skin taking on a reassuring pink tone.

"Heart rate?"

"One hundred and fifty."

"Pili, let's put on a CPAP and put her in the incubator, please."

I look over my mask into her eyes to make her understand that I'm sorry about my earlier tone. It's best to keep Pili happy, otherwise she acts all offended and pays me back by making me wait for the blood work. At least she gets cross with me, which is something in and of itself. For the last few months everyone's been incredibly forgiving when I lose my patience and their indulgence actually makes me more angry and irritable.

As I wait for the incubator, I rub the baby's tiny back sweetly, this time to thank her for making that immense effort to cling to life. But I can't help thinking that, deep down, I'm touching her for some other, more elusive reason too, something to do with the fact that she's still here when Mauro isn't. Because he's not here, Paula. He's gone and, yet he comes to me even here as I'm handling these few grams of gelatinous life.

"Here you go, Mama. Give your daughter a kiss." I bring the baby over to her mother for just a few seconds so they can meet. "She had some trouble breathing but now she's fine. We're going to bring her up to the ICU like we talked about, OK? I'll be back in a little while to explain everything in detail. Don't worry, everything'll be fine."

But I don't promise her anything. Even though the mother's eyes are begging me to give them hope, after Mauro I don't make any promises.

2

Lídia will be here soon, her office hours end at one. I feel a wave of relief, knowing I'll see her. In mere minutes I'll hear her chattering away, plunging me back into normality, just what my body is demanding from me. After the summer holidays, that's the key: getting back into my routine.

I wait for her amid the bustle of the hospital canteen as I move my salad around on the plate. The smell of a huge communal pot of broth is stuck in my nose, sending me back to the school cafeteria, where I hid things I didn't like in the pockets of my uniform or traded in chicken thighs with the hungrier students. The paediatrician ordered my father to make me toast with honey to keep up the battle against my low percentile, which he pointed to with a pencil on that odious growth chart. Honey became a regular part of my diet and of our grey days without Mum, not to sweeten things, but to fatten me up. I read somewhere that an eighty-three-year-old Hindu ascetic had survived without eating or drinking for more than seventy years. A team from the Research and Development branch of India's Ministry of Defence studied him for a couple of weeks. The only contact he had with water was when washing or gargling. The doctor who was conducting the experiment came to the conclusion that if he wasn't obtaining energy from food or water, then it had to be coming from some other source in his environment, such as the sun. When the experiment ended, the yogi returned to his hometown to resume his meditation. It seems he had been blessed by a goddess when he was eight and that allowed him to live without food.

Four days after Mauro's death, and by that I mean literally four days, I had ingested only lime blossom tea; luckily, I'd let my father add some honey from his local beekeeper. Unable to put up a fight, I'd allowed it. I don't know what graph curve he was trying to increase at that point. Once again, my sadness was dripping out in amber tones.

They were apathetic, unreal days, the shock filled everything, there was no space for hunger. I remember my father's firm hand turning the wooden spoon and honey rolling slowly through the slits without dripping. My father is a perfectionist and found it inconceivable that I didn't have a wooden honey spoon. He bought me one. He also organized my cutlery drawer and fixed the door to the pantry where I kept my pots. For a week my father and Lídia took turns, maintaining a constant presence in my home, and I just let them. They filled my fridge with nice things that slowly rotted. Lídia would come at lunchtime or dinnertime to make sure that I ate something and keep me company.

Everyone assumed, during those weeks following the accident, that my stunned gaze, neglected appearance and lowered blinds were due to my sadness over losing the person who'd been my partner for so many years; no one realized that, clinging to the pain of his death, there was another grief, slippery but slow, like a slug able to cover everything—including the other pain—with its viscous trail that gradually saturated everything, ugly, so ugly that all I knew how to do was hide it, I was dying too with the shock of this new shame, even more shocking than the death itself.

I wonder if the two things are somehow linked, if her arrival into my consciousness made him disappear, physically, from my life.

"Come on, Paula, please, at least have the banana. You haven't eaten a thing."

I looked at Lídia, my head tilted to one side, smiling. I had remembered the story of the yogi and was about to make a joke, explaining that a goddess had blessed me and I didn't need food, but seeing the worry on her face I decided to keep it to myself.

"Come on, just a little."

I was sitting in a chair in the kitchen and she stood beside me. We could have been two friends on any old day at lunchtime, in some randomly chosen place where there'd been no deaths of friends or lovers. But the scene's composition was completely deformed. If I bandaged up everything that was hurting inside me, I would have embodied the anachronistic image of a soldier returning from war, mutilated.

Lídia meticulously peeled the banana. I watched her, distracted, and when she offered it to me, stripped and held up in her fingers, we looked into each other's eyes and felt an urge to laugh, without knowing what had brought it on.

"Please, eat. Come on."

"I'm not hungry, Lídia, really. It'll make me feel sick."

"Come on, just the tip…"

We both burst out laughing and I felt my cheeks burning with shame. My laughter calmed her and allowed her to laugh. I needed to calm her first so that she could calm me. The onus of Mauro's sudden death—with bonus cheating—had taught me things others will never know, for instance, that calmness isn't truly possible. And I laughed. I laughed but still wasn't able to eat, I laughed but couldn't sleep, I laughed clammy with cold sweat. I knew that if I stopped abruptly, if I stopped laughing and just told Lídia the truth, that he'd left me, she'd be appalled and the shock of his infidelity would overshadow his death. Crass, clichéd infidelity would take centre stage. But, for now, we were still laughing. Lídia was laughing and I was laughing with her while I sought out her gaze hidden in the folds of her eyelids, wanting to convey it all without having to put it into words; but no, she didn't catch my drift. That you've been dumped, compared to the death of the guy who left you, isn't the sort of news that's easily transmitted in a look.

"Eat, Paula."

I took a bite of the banana just so I wouldn't have to hear her anymore.

"You know that humans have about twenty thousand, five hundred genes and bananas around thirty-six thousand?"

"What are you going on about?"

"That a banana has about fifteen thousand more genes than a human being," I explained to Lídia.

21

"Great, fantastic." She tried on a compassionate expression as she pushed my hair out of my face and put it behind my ear. I'd never felt pity from her before. "Everything's going to be fine, sweetie. You'll get past this."

Deep inside, in silence, I thought, no, I won't.

Soon the sweet, pasty texture of the banana that I was struggling to swallow took on the salty taste of my tears.

"Guess who?" Hands cover my eyes, from behind. I didn't see her coming. I turn and we hug. Lídia is a whirlwind of wild, blonde curls, and a rain of freckles decorates her whole face.

At first we talk a blue streak, competing to get a word in edgewise. We catch up on the details of getting back to work after the summer, then I complain indignantly about the state of the renovations, which are very far along in the newer wing where she works as a paediatrician. I'm forced to work between constricting walls, in spaces that are too compartmentalized, with insufficient light and twisting passageways. All the facilities that the public doesn't see have been left on the back burner, despite their need for an overhaul. Lídia sticks out her tongue at me, to stop my complaining. Our friendship has never been equal. She always imposes herself subtly, but I've accepted it since the very first day, just like I've always accepted that circumstances have moulded me inwards, into myself. Then she tells me about her disappointment with the hotels she stayed in during her trip to Scotland—that the carpets were gross and the food revolting, that they made a mistake with one of the reservations and ended up in a room that was so dirty they decided to sleep in the car, all four of them—and, as if we were still on her parents' roof terrace studying for finals, we put our arms together to compare our tans.

"You look great," she announces with a smile. "These days have done you good."

And I let her believe her own conclusion because I don't feel like talking about me or about the two weeks I spent in Selva de Mar, at my father's house. The supposed tranquillity of life far from the rat race, the pleasure of simple things, the famous inner peace that everyone insisted would do me such good, none of it had worked.

I hadn't been back there since the accident, and with the opaque filter of time, my father's town seemed different, the church bigger and the streets narrower, the church bells had never chimed so loudly nor the laughter of the summer people in the square been so brazen. I'd had it up to here with the calmness, my father's melancholy piano playing, the birds that woke me up at dawn just when I'd managed to fall asleep; I was sick of the internet connection failing, of having to hang off a cliff just to get third-rate phone coverage, and of the games of chess after meals. No, the tranquillity had only set off all my alarms and amplified the questions I was supposedly avoiding during my first vacation without Mauro. So, to keep my conversation with Lídia from turning doleful, I make sure to keep lobbing out questions so she can't question me. After all, a mother just back from a family trip around Europe is always going to have more stories to tell than a single woman whose brilliant summer plan was spending fifteen days in a tiny town whipped by the north wind, surrounded by her father's friends, who are all pushing seventy.

"And how are the girls?"

"Oh man, the girls... you'll see them soon enough. Daniela's unbearable, a textbook teenager, and Martina's following close on her heels: now, when one of them wants a pool day the other wants to go to the beach, and it's like that with everything." She sighs hard before continuing. "I swear, travelling with kids is a real trial. You can't even imagine how many times I wanted to leave them with Toni, sneak off and join you in that small town, sunbathe in the buff all day long, and smoke and drink every night without having to hide."

Why didn't you, I think. Why did you leave me alone for so many days? The adult inside me knows that Lídia is married, that she has daughters, responsibilities, a family to spend her holidays with. The adult bites her tongue and smiles, tells her it wasn't all that, that she's anxious to see the girls, that she bought them some T-shirts, that everything went well in her father's town, same as ever, that her dad is strong as an ox, cooking all day long, and she must have gained at least three kilos.

"And? You must have been popular...?" And then she fixes those blue eyes of hers on me, those eyes that always find you out when you're trying to dodge something. I don't think she was referring to men in particular with that question, just trying to suss out how I was doing.

"With dozens of French tourists." I wave a hand over my body from top to bottom, then extend my arms as if to say, have you seen me lately, do I look like I'm in a state where I could possibly get involved with another human being?

"Well, that's probably better. It's all very recent. Let things settle, so you can think more clearly. Mauro's… it's too soon. I don't know that it's the right moment, Paula."

The right moment for what, I think. Is there some set period of time? In the instruction manual for those left behind does it say anything about how soon you can go out and play without being considered tawdry? But the adult in me just nods her head slightly, while lining up all the cherry tomatoes in the salad on one side of the plate.

* * * * * *

I've read that over the long term our brains employ reconstructions and abstractions to store memories, which is why we can even go to the extreme of producing false ones. I wonder how I can hold on to your memory, intact and in a fair way.

It would be much easier if I could experience those memories in chronological order, but that's not the case. They appear randomly, coming and going in miscellaneous bursts that don't help to give shape to the collection of contrasts that was your life, or your life with me.

You knew how to sew. You would sew on buttons, darn the occasional hole in a sock.

When you couldn't find something and you called out for me to come and help you look, you'd call me Pauli, and I didn't like that but you never stopped doing it.

You would sneeze three times in a row when you got out of bed in the morning. When you called your mother on the phone your tone of voice would change. When you said "Mama" with that childlike ring, I would grab my keys and go out for a walk because I knew you'd give in to whatever she demanded of you. You smelt clean. You didn't wear any cologne, it was a pure scent of warm water and soap.

When you were deep into reading the newspaper you would break biscuits with your tongue against the roof of your mouth. One after the other. At first I found it amusing, but over the years I would nag you about eating so much sugar.

When we made love, just as we were getting started, if I touched you, an ever so slight shiver would run through you, like a tiny shock, like a bittersweet reaction of desire and aversion. It must not have always been that way, but I can't remember how it was at the beginning.

You liked to buy me shoes. I never told you but I usually wasn't crazy about the ones you chose for me. I felt bad about it and would wear them to make you happy. They were shoes for a woman who didn't have my feet, or my style that wasn't really a style. They were shoes for a woman who wasn't me.

Before leaving the house you would kiss me on the forehead, a sincere kiss, filled with tenderness. That's how it always was. Always.

* * * * * *

3

A jar of mayonnaise. Two beers. A vegetable reduced to a wilted stump covered in velvety mould. Two yogurts a week past their use-by date. I grab one. An almost empty jar of bitter orange marmalade, and the electric hum of the refrigerator. That's all. Welcome home.

The red light on the answering machine is blinking. Just one message. For a moment, my heart leaps, but no, it can't be Pep. I don't think I ever gave him my home number. I want to think that he staunchly follows my battle orders, and when someone tells you "Get away from me because we'll hurt each other" there isn't much room for confusion. I'll confess that sometimes I invoke him. Some nights I call out to him silently and beg him to phone me, show some sign of life. A message, an image, any proof he's out there would be fine. Some nights I fall asleep with my phone in my hand, after hours of weighing whether I should tell him things or not, whether it's true that we would be so bad for each other. There are certain moments when I curse his resolve, and others when I can scarcely believe that, at forty-two years old, I've emerged from the ashes looking so childish, so hesitant, so unruly. It's like stumbling around all day long, and often I think that Pep probably doesn't even remember my name anymore.

So if there's only one message, it's definitely not from him. In fact, I can only imagine it's from my father—he's the sole reason I keep that dusty, anachronistic device in the house, sitting there impassive beside the television. My father not only leaves me voice messages; he even plays his piano compositions into it. I still have relics on there, several minutes long, and I could never bear to part with them in the technological shift. No matter what time I get home, it's always blinking, letting me know there's some music to listen to, or his voice curious to hear my take. It's sometimes better to ring him back right away, otherwise he has a tendency to insist. There are some restless, insatiable personality types who should never be allowed to retire.

I press the button and, as expected, his voice fills the room. As I listen between spoonfuls of yogurt, I raise the blinds on the back balcony to let in the light and air the place out a little.

"You must have just arrived... I hope you didn't hit a lot of traffic. I ran into Pepi and she says hi. She says if she'd known you were in town she would have loved to see you, give you a hug... Oh, Paula! You left that piece of cake that Maria brought you yesterday, here on the counter in the kitchen... I just wanted to wish you a good return to work. That's all... And eat, you hear me? Love you."

I stop with my mouth half open, immediately repulsed. I throw out the yogurt. The image of the cake in the tupperware from Maria at Can Rubiés makes me retch. I saw it in the kitchen this morning before I left my father's house.

29

I had it in my hands, in fact, but I put it down on the marble counter because the container had the same musty smell as Maria's breath.

"We have to be strong, sweetie. You're very young. You have to remake your life."

She just blurted it out last Tuesday afternoon, when my father and I went to see her and she offered us some coffee. I know my father has good intentions, visiting neighbours when they're sick or have lost a family member. I think it has to do with his obsession with wanting to feel that he belongs in that town where he's been spending more and more time; I've never seen him do it in Barcelona, except with close friends or family members, and despite everything his city ways show through in the details: he writes down the visits in a calendar and he even gets dressed up for them. On Tuesday morning, while we were having breakfast in the courtyard, an alarm went off on his phone. He wiped his lips with a napkin and, still chewing, informed me:

"Maria, at noon. We have to hurry if we want to take a dip at Port de la Selva before we stop by to give her our condolences."

I stared at him, sceptical, and said there was no way I was going with him to Maria's house, that paying my condolences to people I don't know wasn't in my summer plans.

"But she knows you. If you come with me, I'll make angler fish with clams tonight for dinner."

—

30

No one in that town knows that Mauro left me a few hours before he died. Not even my father, although he was aware we were going through a really rough patch. It was autumn, but we were still in short sleeves. Mauro and I had had a big argument; I'd bought plane tickets for the long weekend in November and the dates weren't good for him because of some work conflict. I'd told him that he couldn't complain I never surprised him, and that led to shouting and slammed doors. He told me to go screw myself and I snapped that, with him, that was probably my best option. Half an hour later I met my father to go with him to the dermatologist. They had to remove some moles from his back and, being a wimp, he'd asked me to go home with him after the procedure, which was a very simple one. While we waited for the nurse to call him in, even though I knew he wouldn't help me because he'd never known how to, I got carried away in the weakness of the moment and I let him know that Mauro and I weren't getting along well, without going into details. My voice trembled and then he said that bit about the bad season. That was what he called it. A bad season, Paula, you'll see how things will be good again in the springtime. It happens to all couples. And with that facile view of time's healing powers and two pats on the shoulder he considered the problem solved. Inside my head I laughed at my own naivety and told them both to take a long walk off a short pier. Problems removed as easily as moles. The springtime.

My father would have been terribly sorry to hear that we'd separated after all those years, so much so that I imagine he would've struggled to come up with an explanation to give his friends that would soften the blow of having an old maid for a daughter. He liked to say things like "My son-in-law is an editor" or "There's an interview with my son-in-law in *La Vanguardia* today" or "My son-in-law got the Noisette rose bush on my eastern wall to flower". They truly appreciated each other, and created their own communion around the legal family we never were, that I always stood in the way of. Calling him his "son-in-law" gave him slightly more posses- sion. "Paula's staying with me for a few days. My son-in-law had an accident. He's dead."

The fact that Mrs Maria knew who I was when I didn't know her could only mean that my father hadn't hesitated to introduce me in his circle as Paula, poor thing, who lost her spouse in an accident. In a way, it's easier to explain your daughter's change in relationship status when there's a death involved, rather than opening the door to discussions about couples today, with so much freedom and so little energy for fixing things when they aren't perfect. Death fixes the irrep- arable; it's unalterable and distorts everything. It changed Mauro and placed him in the realm of the saints and the innocent. Death is like springtime.

My father and Maria spoke in phrases that trailed off, almost like something out of a phrasebook. There is a specific lan- guage for talking about the dead, an inventory of aphorisms using sounds that waver between respect and fear. I watched them from the doorway, avoiding a scent that floated in the air, a mix of bitter quince and freshly sliced, cured sausage, anxious for the coffee to be ready, hoping that the coffeepot would explode and we could run away and not have to sit down around that table covered in sticky oilcloth, where there must still have been prints from Mrs Maria's dead husband's plump fingers.

It was 26 August and she was wearing a long-sleeved black cardigan, a skirt to her ankles and some winter house slippers, with no back and a slight heel. I wore flat sandals made of two scant strips of leather, clearly marking our differences. We aren't the same woman and as such we don't share the same pain, despite which we've both been recruited by grief, like an infectious agent with the ability to reproduce and be transmitted irrespective of the wishes of those left behind. My pain is mine and I don't want her coming anywhere near it.

Without knowing how, I was sitting next to her, forcing a smile and trying not to think about the edge of the oilcloth lightly brushing my thighs, when all of a sudden the bubbling of the coffeepot declared that there was no escape. Mrs Maria got up, serenely turned off the flame, and pulled three mugs that looked like toys from a faded Formica cabinet that released a gust of stale air into the room. That was when, in the midst of a silence broken only by the kitchen clock, she got very close to me, too close, so close she forced me to shut my eyes, and she said it.

"We have to be strong, sweetie. You're very young. You have to remake your life."

33

I don't want Maria, or her halitosis, anywhere near me. I don't want cake. I don't want to hear more predictions about my future. I don't want to share in her strength, much less for her to identify with me. My pain is mine and the only possible unit for measuring or calibrating it is the intimacy of everything that comprised the how. How I loved him, how he loved me. How we were, uniquely, no longer us and, therefore, how I could uniquely grieve him.

It seemed my father realized how the scene had upset me, and that very night, as I was sitting on a deck chair under the fig tree, he came outside, turned off the porch light and asked me to prick up all my senses. At the house in Selva de Mar that he'd bought with much effort, saving and pride, the small garden's low ivy-covered wall borders a forested area that marks the end of the town. When you sit there in silence there are soon a multitude of sounds: crickets, the buzzing of moths and mosquitoes, leaves cradled by the breeze, the murmur of the creek that runs right through the centre of town, the flapping of a bat's wings and, every once in a long while, the majestic hooting of an owl. Over fifteen days I only heard it three times. My father told me that I wouldn't see it, that since he's been summering in that house, all those years, he's only very sporadically glimpsed the owl flying away. He mentioned, off the cuff, that in ancient times, owls represented the union between three worlds: the underworld, the visible world and the heavens. According to what he said, for the ancient Egyptians, but also for the Celts and the Hindus, the owl was a totem that protected the souls of the dead. He lowered his head slightly and put his hands in the pockets of his shorts when he said "dead". I warned him not to continue, that even though I was only a few months away from turning forty-three, Mauro's death had me easily frightened and even the esoteric made me uncomfortable lately. He laughed, ran an arm over my shoulder, and pulled me towards him.

"Oh, come on, Paula. Turn it around. Owls can also belong to the moon, they're messengers of secrets and omens. Look at it like this: the owl brings wisdom, freedom and change."

Then he kissed my hair and said good night. I could only squeeze his hand, unable to say anything, overcome by the emotion of his gesture.

The black sky sparkling with stars fell on me with its own weight, the infinite weight of everything that does not belong to me, everything that I do not know. I don't believe in such things and feel much safer in the world of logic and science; but the conversation stays with me and my father's words resonate deep inside, leaving me unsettled. I take for granted that Mauro's soul's already protected by my silence, and in any case, if it's about handing out totems, I'm the one who deserves one, to support me and push me to follow my path.

Death makes me angry. Since he's no longer here, death irritates me, exasperates me with its insolence and lack of shame, with how it harbours Mauro and for how alive it is.

I open the door to my terrace, determined to expunge those vexing images from my mind, but August has wreaked havoc on my oasis. The ferns have become a brownish swirl of dried leaves, the calla lilies are more yellow than green, the gardenias have aphids. The ground is covered in dried leaves. I take stock. Only the thatch palms, spider plants and the orange tree have survived.

"Let's put in thatch palms, Paula, trust me, they never die."

We were right here when he said that, a thousand years ago now, with an empty apartment and high hopes. We looked out with satisfaction at that huge terrace, like our future, with no storm clouds on the horizon. No one warned us that the thatch palms would outlive him. No one told us that I would be the one who had to take care of his plants now.

"Good morning, Paula!"

I hear Thomas's unmistakably American-accented Spanish, from the apartment upstairs. My neighbour is at the window smoking a cigarette.

"When did you get back? I missed you!"

"Ten minutes ago, and look at all this," I say, pointing to the plants. "Was there a nuclear war while I was away and no one told me?"

"Next year, ask me to water them for you."

But they're Mauro's plants and Mauro would never have asked him to take care of them over the summer. I'm sure Thomas would do it, with the same care and patience he displays with me, yet, despite trusting him, I can't bring myself to admit I forgot to turn on the automatic watering system and didn't realize until I'd already got through kilometres of August Friday traffic on the motorway and, by that point, wasn't up for turning around. That deep inside I thought: Fuck him. But now, here, surrounded by derelict, ailing plants, I feel like a wretched human being. The Mauro I fell in love with believed that we are just one part of this planet's creation, that all the world's flora and fauna deserve the same attention we devote to humans. He used to say that we are here to reproduce, like cats, like whales, like bacteria, like plants. One evening, when perhaps we were already a triangle and I didn't know it, I remember having criticized him, saying he had better intuition for when an orchid was in danger of dehydration than for when I was in the mood for sex. He looked at me, hurt. I'd like to forget that look, I'd like to take back some of the things we said to each other.

It's childish to think that Mauro was still somewhere when he'd been reduced to two and a half kilos of ash, but if he, or his supposed spirit, were anywhere on this planet, it would be here on this terrace, among these plants.

"Will you invite me in for lunch, Thomas? All I have are out-of-date yogurts, so anything's fine."

He turns to glance inside the house, and in a very soft voice he lets me know that he's not alone. "Tomorrow would be better…" He winks at me and blows me a kiss. "Happy to see you!" he adds in English.

I glimpse someone with long blonde hair moving in the half-light. I smile, slowly. Looks like there is life on earth.

—

With my hands on my hips I survey the damage. I head over to what's left of his plants and murmur to them: "I have no intention of letting you die, you bastards. I'm not Mrs Maria. My name is Paula Cid and I can breathe life into anything."

* * * * * *

Nineteen Eighty-Four. It's hard to believe, I know, but it was George Orwell who allowed me access to your phone that first night you were no longer alive. Maybe I'd seen you type it once and had subconsciously memorized the code, but I like to think I won that hand because of your predictability. You and your books, you weren't so exceptional, you see? Second try. It wasn't that hard. The first attempt was the secret number on your credit card. It didn't work. We'd been a couple long enough that we were used to excessive openness, to invading each other's private spaces, like bathrooms and credit cards. And we'd also had time to develop an intuition solid enough to predict each other's movements without even being aware we were doing it. After all, you intuit everything in the same way, whether it's a bad mood or a PIN code.

Then I remembered, one Sunday after lunch, you and Nacho dismissing the latest novel by a British author you published in translation. You'd had very high hopes, you'd invested a lot, but you couldn't believe how weak the material you'd received was. You were even considering suggesting the editor cut out some chapters. The languid sweetness of Sunday afternoon and the bottle of Grand Marnier had you both anaesthetized, laughing and slurring your words.

Nacho jokingly suggested being subtler and reminding the author of George Orwell's six rules of writing. I was waiting in the kitchen with Montse, helping her tidy everything up and impatient to get home so I could shower before my shift. I wasn't feeling very well at all and I whispered in your ear to please, wrap it up. You nodded without even looking at me or asking me what was wrong. You made that lateral movement with your eyes, fleetingly, as you thought up your response to your friend, who was goading you on, saying sure, maybe *Nineteen Eighty-Four* was the harshest critique of Western capitalism, but to him it wasn't Orwell's best work, not by a long chalk. You must not even remember that scene, not because you're dead and the dead don't remember, but because sometimes, when you were alive, if you got excited about something, you would make me disappear, to be left alone with the person you were talking to and with your selfishness. You didn't hear my pleading. And I hated George Orwell, or maybe I hated you. I asked you for the car keys and left alone without saying a word. When I came out of the shower wrapped in a towel and my hair still dripping, I went into your office and ripped one of the corners of the film poster for Michael Radford's *1984*. I'd always thought it was awful. I went to work, leaving a ton of wet footprints I knew wouldn't be dry by the time you came home. I'm no good at covering my guilty tracks either.

1-9-8-4, I ran my finger over the screen and the curtain lifted on your life without me. You should know that I didn't pry into everything until after the funeral, snooping before you'd been laid to rest seemed incredibly disrespectful, and, when I did, it was in small bites so I wouldn't choke. So I could pretend that I was spying on you as if you were still a little bit alive. So that "Doing it with you in restaurant loos between the main course and dessert takes ten years off my age every time" and the request to "Wear that outrageous green G-string again tonight, I'll be rock hard all day just thinking about it", those I didn't read until later, when I had already found out about so many other things. Things that turned you into a man I could scarcely recognize.

The night you died, though, amid the emptiness of the kitchen, with the hum of the fridge as the only indication that all of it was really happening, I read just one message, the last one you had sent her, right after having dinner with me and shaking up my whole world. When we hadn't even buried you yet, I recognized her name and I read the last words you sent her, the last words you wrote: "I told her, Carla. It's done."

You were dead and my first thought was that you were pussywhipped.

* * * * * *

4

When I got there, at two forty-five, Marta and Vanesa were already putting on their white coats in front of the lockers, laughing hysterically.

"Good afternoon, ladies. Looks like this shift is promising."

They soon pull me along in their joyful wake, telling me about a new store that sells sex toys on the street level of Vanesa's building, in Horta. They try to convince me to go there with them one day. Vanesa and Marta are the junior doctors on my team and I love them. I've tried to limit my affection for them because I know they'll be leaving in a matter of months, but it's been impossible. They're so young and life looks so good on them...

Marta turns to make sure no one is watching and opens up her shirt to show us her new bra. We tell her it's fabulous and make all sorts of saucy comments. I think it looks run-of-the-mill and even vulgar, but I don't say that to her. I have the feeling I'm getting old and if I play along with them I'm somehow keeping a toe in their world. But the irresistible effervescence of their late twenties plainly leaves me out of a competition I desperately want to be in. I can't help looking at Marta's firm, pert breasts, their Cooper's ligaments at the height of their tautness, and I observe them like someone admiring an icon of desire, fascination and sensuality. I can scarcely hear them laughing because suddenly, without warning, Pep comes into my thoughts and, like a spark, incites a memory.

He placed an index finger on my bra strap and pulled it down very slowly, tracing the rounded shape of my shoulder. First one, then the other. In recent years, I'd only been with Mauro. The few men I'd slept with before him were just a game I played, alternating them with exams and anatomy textbooks.

The thought of Pep still gives me a thrill of novelty and payback, but I pushed him aside with the pragmatism of someone turning off a tap. Pleasure that appears just four weeks after losing your partner forever feels too bold, and as soon as it's over you have to keep it an absolute secret. You have to scrub your body very hard with a loofah glove to get it off your skin, you have to scrub until it's red and raw with pain and shame. "Keep away from me because we'll hurt each other" seemed like the easiest words. I don't know why I'm still hoping to hear from him. If I were in his place, I wouldn't ever want to see me again.

"Isn't that right, Paula? You tell her, she won't listen to me!"

I don't know what Marta's talking about. I lost the thread of the conversation at some point and, besides, I'm suddenly in a bad mood.

When Santi enters the office with a serious air about him, they both straighten up. Marta coughs slightly and adjusts her white coat, and Vanesa quickly closes her locker.

During the shift change, as we sit at the round table, reviewing the patients' charts, I focus on Santi's hands, enormous and crowned with a tangle of white hairs like the fibrous wool of Icelandic sheep. He has an old man's hands, disproportionate, that grow bigger as they approach the tiny bodies of our babies in the NICU. I imagine him at home doing small things with those massive hands: peeling a clove of garlic, braiding cornrows into his granddaughters' hair, plucking a few hairs from between his brows with tweezers, and knotting his tie each morning. I think those big-boned hands must get in the way of things. Suddenly, I imagine his hands on the breasts of his wife, Anna Maria. I imagine them in bed. Her with her perfect bun and that violet eyeshadow, so eighties, and him with those old gorilla hands dominating in the lotus position. Do they still sleep together? There's the lingering cliché that men think about sex twenty-four hours a day and women only rarely, but lately I can't stop thinking about Mauro and Carla, about their bodies together, alive and warm. I anxiously read their chats whenever I feel like it, I've learnt them by heart, and now their sex is mine, coming to light when I want and only then, and on the days when I'm feeling more compassionate I'm able to think of her and how she must feel without him, and I imagine her sitting on the floor with a pair of scissors cutting up her outrageous green G-string and I think, *deal with it, doll*, and the hurt bounces back in my face and reminds me that not only do I know exactly how long it's been since those two were in bed together, but I also know how many months it's been since I last was in bed with Pep. The hurt pounds me when I total up how long Mauro and I were together without passion. Empty sex. Where does all the unconsumed desire go? Does it transform like energy passing into less useful forms? And what's more useful for remaining alive than the ghost of desire? Just look at Vanesa and Marta, bursting with life when they come in here each day, gleaming, levitating, they're pure glitter. They always say that getting laid is easy, and I pretend not to be interested as I administer ibuprofen intravenously to some teensy infant and watch them out of the corner of my eye, overflowing with envy, and I can't work up the guts to ask them how, where, and if they think I could too, in my circumstances, how can I strip away everything and grasp that the opposite of death is desire? Ghosts inside my distraught brain. I still have to tame them. Death forces a certain solemnity, an inactivity, a renegotiation with every single thing that gave life meaning before, in order to adapt to life now.

Santi catches me observing his hands and shoots me a withering look.

"And what do you suggest, Dr Cid?" he challenges.

I feel like a little girl being scolded for being naughty, my cheeks burn, but I force myself to adopt a convincing expression and look at the junior doctors instead of at him.

"I feel confident about it. Mahavir's been in a stable condition for two weeks now, despite the bronchopulmonary dysplasia that has me worried. For the moment, I would keep up the respiratory support but try to lower the pressure."

Then I seek out his gaze, haughtily, to show him that he has no reason to doubt me, that I'm on top of everything and not missing a beat. But before he leaves, he calls me into the small back office, the one with opaque windows. He is both tall and old and the room shrinks when he's in it.

"Have a seat, Paula, please."

"Santi, Marta's expecting me in HDU, I don't want to make her wait because…" He silences me, trapping my scrawny hand between his immense ones.

"Paula, how's everything going?"

His tone takes me back to the French classes I took when I was younger, to those dialogues they had us read out loud in pairs. There was that theatricality, those exaggerated accents that turned it all into a farce.

"Vous avez choisi?"

"Une salade et une eau minérale, s'il vous plaît."

"Et pour monsieur?"

"Un sandwich et un café. Merci."

If Mauro were alive and someone asked me how everything was going, I would just say "Doing fine, how about yourself?" like all mortals do, and then we'd change the subject because we'd know, more or less accurately, that, really, as long as we're alive we're OK. We'd know that it's just a simple question, a placeholder, a conversational gambit, but Mauro isn't alive and the responses expected from me demand I show fragility, humility.

"Good, how are things with you?"

Santi softens his gaze to indicate his rejection of that reply, relaxing his shoulders as if he wants me to understand that we're sitting here because he worries about me, to remind me that he's all ears. He doesn't realize that I interpret his gesture as a selfish act, designed merely to fulfil his duty. That kindness warps into something self-serving. Everybody knows, deep down, what my situation is. Why do they have to ask? "How's everything going?" is a completely absurd question to ask someone who's recently lost the man who dumped her.

"What now?" would undoubtedly be a more appropriate question. "What now, Paula?" and I would answer that I didn't know, that all I'd come up with so far was breathing and working.

"Paula, listen. We've known each other for many years and I know everything that's happened these last few months has really affected you. Of course it has. With good reason. I know how much you loved Mauro. You're a strong woman and you'll get past this, but remember that if you need to take some time for yourself, you have every right. You're an indispensable part of our team, one of the finest physicians we have on staff, but there are priorities, and if you need to take some time off, I have no objections. We just need some advance warning to prepare, both for you and for us."

"I'm fine, Santi, really."

"Paula, sometimes it seems we can just fill in the void with sand, tamp it down and continue on our path. But you shouldn't hesitate to ask for some time to recover."

I hate the rhythm these conversations have, their sustained silences I'm forced to somehow muddle through. If I don't stand up right now I'll fall into that void, or I'll shout or I'll vomit. How dare he lecture me? Mauro's dead but I'm the one who has to shoulder his tragedy, he died and now I have to reinvent myself? Cuckolded, alone and with homework to do.

"Santi, I appreciate it, really, but there's no need."

"Very well, I trust you. But give it some thought, OK?"

I stand up and put the chair back in its place. I don't look him in the eye as I turn tail, furious. The ease with which people pronounce sentences about my future irritates me no end. There are condolence prophets who should think about throwing in the towel. I appreciate Santi, I would even say I love him, like a father, like a grandfather, for everything he's taught me, all those secrets not found in medical textbooks. But in moments like this I hate him for insisting on making me feel so vulnerable and bringing a lump to my throat here, in my work environment, the only setting where I still feel I have some confidence. Not here, Santi, for heaven's sake, not here.

The shift is a calm one. The twins born last night are making steady progress, and Mahavir, poor little thing, continues on, in as delicate a state as ever. He was born at just five hundred grams, his Indian blood running through every tiny vein in his tiny body. After months here he now weighs 2,100 grams, and it seems he's finally adapting to the treatment, even though he still needs oxygen. But Pili, who's been working as a nurse in this hospital for more than thirty years, wrinkles her nose every time she opens up his incubator to attend to him.

"This boy, Paula…" she says to me in Spanish, this time making a face and shaking her head.

"Pili, can I ask you for a favour?"

"Of course." She hasn't turned towards me, she still has her hand inside the incubator as she skilfully changes his nappy.

"Would you please stop making negative comments in front of Mahavir, or any of the other babies for that matter?"

She turns, surprised. She looks at me for a few seconds, her eyes wide, and then continues with her tasks, facing the incubator, offended, not saying a word, but working impeccably as always. I immediately feel regret, because Pili is a true professional and adores the babies. I know that when she has doubts about one of them she's not usually wrong and that's why I can't stand to listen to it. I don't know how to explain to her that Mahavir is important to me, that I need his mother's stories about Bangalore that transport me far far away. She's promised me that if I ever make a trip to India, they'll treat me like a queen, and maybe because I have only hypothetical plans, I cling to the possibility of a colourful voyage and the dim excitement it awakens in me. I don't know how to explain to Pili how strange things are sometimes and how I can't stop thinking about the fact that two unconnected elements could be related forevermore by chance. That's what's really going on with me, it's not her but me and my fixation with the fact that the day Mahavir's mother was admitted, long before he was born, when he was just explicit, formal information in the mouths of obstetricians and neonatologists, was the day Mauro ended forever more.

"Pili." I touch her shoulder but she doesn't turn. I try a second time. Nothing. She is one of the proudest and most stubborn women I know.

"Mahavir, sweetie, can you pull out all those tubes for a moment and tell Pili to forgive me?"

She closes the doors to the incubator slowly and turns with a sly smile. Her broad waist and plump curves are imposing, reminiscent of an early twentieth-century sculpture or a representation of Mother Earth. Someone you could wrap yourself around every night.

"I'm sorry. I don't know what came over me," I say sincerely.

She lightly brushes my shoulder and heads off, loaded down with bottles of milk and nappies as she mutters, "My grandmother always said that it's better to wait tenderly for the bad stuff, when the bad stuff's so bad you can see it coming a mile off."

5

Pep burst into my life with the force of a hurricane.

"I heard you on your phone, speaking a familiar language. Hi, I'm Pep."

The warmth of hearing Catalan there, my own little native tongue amid the alienation of a vast international airport, pulled me from my grey disappointment at the announcement of the cancelled flight. The familiarity of the everyday in those few simple words sounded like a haven in that hostile environment.

The blue neon light illuminating the airport bar had me thinking about the heat source in the new incubators in the NICU. Thirty-two degrees centigrade to keep the newborns' bodies stable at thirty-six or thirty-seven with constant relative humidity. Of all the incubators in the unit, the oldest one is my favourite. Londres, I call it: my misty London. The new ones are perfectly crafted spacecraft bathed by stellar bluish light, but they lack the nostalgic mist that pearls up in drops on the outside. Pep's unexpected entrance dispersed the objective thoughts that kept me tied to the conference.

At that point I didn't yet know that he would be the one who shattered the impartiality that had guided me through the years—based on my experiences, my pragmatic observation of the facts at hand—and that our encounters and my memories of them would be enough to smooth me like a pebble, a pebble that was now washed up on the shore by that oblivion I myself had forced on him, and which, actually, he seemed to be just fine with.

The airport in Amsterdam had ground to a halt. It had been snowing hard for days across northern Europe, tons of flights had been cancelled and most of the passengers were stranded overnight at the terminal, where advertising panels featuring white sand beaches and tropical forests decorated a space and time frozen in a mocking fourth dimension.

I was in a bad mood because of the cancelled flight and tired after two days at the conference, and even though I was denying it to myself, I was upset by the knowledge that, when I got home, despite the punctuality or lack thereof of any flight, Nacho would have already picked up the last two boxes of Mauro's things, books and plants that seemed to reproduce by mitotic division. Our home had been filled with them, books and plants scattered like spores.

"Are you sure you want me to have all this, Paula?"

I nodded, with a scarcely audible yes.

In those last boxes, I'd placed his gardening tools, the gloves that had moulded to his hands, his metal watering can. I'd piled them up beside the door because my pragmatism couldn't conceive of any other place. Nacho had already made a first trip a few days after the accident to take the bulk of Mauro's belongings; he was the only one who knew about the situation with Carla and he didn't have the guts to question me when I told him to just take all of Mauro's stuff, and then let his family know that if they needed anything they should ask him for it.

"That's going to seem very strange to them, Paula."

But at that point I'd stopped caring about everything and everyone and I perceived his family as all of a piece, as a stagnant pool of water with weedy roots stretching down deep. I felt that emptying myself of him was the only way I could take in some air. I was drowning. Drowning in pain. I still didn't know then that it didn't matter how many boxes I filled, or how diligently I wiped away every trace of Mauro, every cinema stub, every razor. I didn't know that, despite all my efforts at impeccably eradicating his trail, he would inhabit unexpected places, in the spontaneous whiff of someone turning a corner behind me or in some talk-show guest's nervous pushing up of his glasses, Mauro's exact gesture there in the middle of some televised conversation. He persisted in a resilient, pervasive network intent on reminding me that he'd been alive for forty-three years, many of them by my side, in this space we'd called our home.

I didn't tell Nacho that I'd kept his spare glasses, the ones with the plastic frames. Dark Havana, Mauro had announced when he wore them for the first time, and I had laughed heartily. What colour is dark Havana? Dark Havana is this brown. That brown is regular old brown. No, it's dark Havana, Paula, I swear. And we had hugged and I'd said, whatever, they look great on you. And I can still feel the warmth in that hug, his clean scent even after a whole day at work, lunch and meetings infusing the cotton of his shirt, the smell of a neat man with well-trimmed fingernails. The smell of a living man. I also kept all his notepads and the green wool jumper we bought in Reykjavik. I thought, one day maybe you'll hug that, Paula, and it's there in the drawer, with his ID card, his yellow international vaccination certificate, and his passport, which he didn't need for his final voyage.

A month later, those two boxes were still in the hallway. They irritated me. Just seeing them there. Hate and love sometimes lump together like beads of mercury, and the amalgam exudes a feeling that's heavy and toxic and strangely wistful. That's what's irritating. The yearning despite it all. The two boxes were the last anchor, a small memory made of flora and literature.

Pep extended a hand after introducing himself amid the noise of the terminal. I considered it for a few moments, confused. So it was true, spontaneity does exist, a stranger can appear out of nowhere at a crowded airport bar, and interact with a subdued woman who's just finished making a call to cancel a work meeting.

"Paula," I answered. How does a person modulate their voice to play that game?

He smiled and dimples appeared on his cheeks.

"I don't believe you. You don't look like a Paula."

"Really? Well, you definitely look like a Pep." Seemed I was making a pretty good job of this banter, for a novice.

He laughed and looked at the herbal infusion I hadn't taken a sip of yet. He pointed to it with one finger and wrinkled his nose.

"Are you going to drink that? I was about to order a glass of wine. Will you join me?"

I shrugged.

"We'll have two glasses of this wine here, please," Pep said to the waiter, pointing to the menu but still speaking in Catalan.

"Excuse me, sir?" he replied in English.

Pep pulled an exaggerated face, eyes wide to mock the linguistic confusion, then ordered the wine again in excessively nasal English. I giggled slightly, something I recognized as a dormant response in my body. He talked about wines and cellars, of grapes local to different regions and denominations of origin while I calculated how many hours of sleep I could fit in before my shift if I managed to get to Barcelona by 10 a.m. Suddenly I found him boring. Too theatrical, too rehearsed, too easy. I cut him off without thinking twice and left some money on the bar.

"I have to go. I have to make a call. Nice to meet you though."

He just nodded goodbye. His entire being took on a disappointed expression, erasing all traces of the playacting that game required, and that was when I saw him without filters, one dimple here and another there. His black eyes were smiling despite my abruptness, and sparked a thousand possibilities. And then I thought about Carla, about those first few chat lines, the oldest messages I'd found between her and Mauro, imbued with the thrill of conquest, with over-the-top perfume, with smudged lipstick, butterflies in the stomach, and the bold freedom of annexing even the smallest, most everyday part of what belonged to me, loosening his tie, maybe wiping a crumb from the corner of his lips while we were deciding whether or not to freeze the leftover broth. All that had been mine. Then a switch inside me flipped and I forced myself to get swept up in the power of a stranger's invitation at a bar. He seemed to sense my wavering and threw out a line again.

"If I stop talking about wine, will you stay, even just for a little while?"

We drank more wine, it was snowing hard outside. The flakes fell obliquely against the streetlights. The terminal felt hermetic, as if I was inside a snow globe—something I'd always wanted and never had. It's the sort of thing you'd be embarrassed to ask someone to bring you back from a trip. All of a sudden it seemed the terminal was spinning, as if someone had started shaking the snow globe.

"I need to go to the loo. Can I trust you with my things, or are you the type to rob me and run off?" I asked, managing a playful tone.

"Don't worry. I'll be waiting here. Go ahead." He looked at me with a calculating expression. He was studying me, deciding what to make of my thin body, my tired face—weighed down by things he couldn't imagine—and my absurd, tipsy banter.

"Keep your belongings with you at all times," I joked in English as I staggered off.

He laughed, still sober. I was feeling quite drunk. My reserve had vanished with three glasses of wine and I was carried away on a blend of exaltation and inebriation.

Washing my face in the bathroom, I felt pleasantly dizzy, exultant even. But I didn't dare to look into my eyes in the mirror. I didn't want to see myself reflected back, didn't want to see any dark circles, or the shadow that seemed to have granted me a brief reprieve.

The boxes must be gone from the hallway. Maybe Carla had asked Nacho for some clothes, a scarf, anything that still held particles of my man—not hers. The game Pep was suggesting was one I'd never played before, and it seemed like the perfect revenge. I combed my hair and touched up my make-up, avoiding the mirror's shadow. The wine took care of directing the movements of my limbs. An older woman, tiredness stamped on her face and a pair of furry boots on her feet, came out of a stall and gave me a dirty look as she washed her hands at the next basin, or maybe I imagined it and I was the one punishing myself in anticipation. She left, muttering something in a language I didn't recognize, shuffling those big bear feet.

When I got back to the bar, Pep was still there.

"Here, this is for you. A souvenir." He handed me something small, inside a plastic airport bag.

I always feel shy when someone surprises me pleasantly, and as the feeling grew inside me it attenuated the alcohol's effect.

"Really? You shouldn't have…"

"Hush, just open it."

I didn't dare look at him as I carefully extracted a small box from the bag. Inside it was a snow globe with a snow-man, resting on a pedestal with a crooked sticker that read "Amsterdam". It was crudely made, with cheap materials and paint that was too glossy. The snowman had a decadent, sad smile that dangerously shifted my mood and the fake snow didn't fall with the slow, elegant cadence of the glass snow globes I'd always longed for. It was a shoddy version of my wish. But I felt I had to look into his eyes, gratefully.

"Touchée," I said, a blithe lie.

I shook the globe a couple of times and we watched how the snow fell.

"One last drink and I'll leave you in peace, OK?" I pleaded. Suddenly I wanted him in a banal, rudimentary way.

He told me he was a carpenter but that what he liked best was cooking. I answered that I was a neonatologist and what I liked best was being a neonatologist.

"I've never had a glass of wine with an expert in miniature babies before."

"I never wanted to fool around with someone who makes tables and chairs before."

He looked at me with wide eyes, pulling his head back slightly, pleasantly surprised. I was doing his work for him.

I couldn't believe I'd said those words out loud, to a stranger. It felt good, releasing a pressure in my chest I hadn't realized I was carrying. Sure I was blushing, I looked down at the tips of my shoes. He lifted my face, taking me by the chin.

"Should we leave?"

The taxi line was impossible. Yet suddenly, in an inexplicable leap in time brought on by the alcohol, we were somehow sharing a cab with two Italian women who were in Amsterdam for their honeymoon. We were moving very slowly because the traffic was chaotic. There was dirty snow by the sides of the road, and the flashing blue light and siren of a police car parked a few metres ahead plunged everything outside the vehicle into a state of alarm and made the whole scene unreal. One of the Italian women was insisting that I looked like Laura Antonelli. Pep googled the actress and nodded, looked at me again and smiled genially. One dimple here, one dimple there. He seemed laid-back, I was trembling with cold and nervousness, Mauro was dead, Carla was alone, and the boxes were gone from the hallway.

The Italian women dropped us in front of a hotel right near the airport, Pep gave them money, it was all weird, like the fragmented memory of a dream. When we said goodbye to the newlyweds, we hugged as if we'd known each other all our lives. The taxi headed off, tracing an illusory wake of happiness while the snow continued to fall on our heads, covering everything, the airport, Amsterdam, Holland, the Netherlands, northern Europe and that universe of mine that was only just beginning.

It was Pep who spoke at the reception desk. He asked me for my boarding pass.

"The airline will take care of the cost," he said happily.

When I gave it to him, he lightly touched the tips of my fingers.

"Your hands are freezing, Paula. Give me a few seconds and we'll have you all warmed up." He winked at me and smiled mischievously. His lips gleamed red and I didn't want him anymore.

I tucked a lock of hair behind my ears and put my gloves back on, not knowing what to do with my hands, or with that game that grew old so quickly. Suddenly my father came into my head, the advice he would give me when I started staying out late, sometimes all night. The next morning we would have breakfast together and he'd butter the toast very slowly, with a parsimony that drove me up the wall. Without asking me how my night had gone, he would speak in an didactic tone about relationships, about the consequences they could have at my age, but he never judged me, he encouraged me to ask him anything at all, and he often and persistently reminded me that I should always demand respect. I never asked him a thing. I hadn't known my mother well, but I was aware that along with her had vanished the possibility of female complicity so evidently missing in those failed conversations with my dad. There were libraries I could consult, and girls at my high school who were much more daring than I was, and with that I had enough, with that and the certainty that I was entering the adult world with the same solitude I'd always had as my companion.

It was unnerving to find myself thinking about my father in those circumstances, about to embark on a spontaneous fling. It was inappropriate, childish, and only made the situation stranger, multiplying the guilt hammering at me: he's only been dead for a little over a month, Paula. And when I thought about a month, I saw a calendar divided up into four weeks, the phases of the moon and the bank holidays marked in red. I felt an urge to run away quickly, the angst of wrongdoing.

I watched as the young woman at the reception desk handed Pep a key card, he seemed relaxed and happy. She looked up from the desk, for just a moment, an accidental glance, but it landed on me. I had the feeling that not only were everyone's eyes on me, but that they all knew what I was going to do.

I took a deep breath, heading towards the revolving door as I tried to persuade myself that I wanted to do what was about to happen. There, standing at the reception desk, still covered in icy snowflakes that were gradually dampening my wool gloves and reaching my skin, the effect of the wine was barely perceptible and I was starting to doubt my bravery of just hours earlier, as Pep nodded to let me know we could go to the room.

We went up, plunged into the sterile silence of the lift. He took my hand in his. A big, rough, new hand. From the wood, I thought. I didn't know anything about wood. I was in a hotel lift holding a carpenter's hand and all I knew about him was his name.

We went into the room, the wall-to-wall carpet swallowing up our timid footsteps. There we were, in a standard room, with the standard smells and sounds of all standard hotel rooms, and yet, at the same time, the mere fact of my being there turned it into an extraordinary space that reminded me what I had come there to do.

Pep looked out of the window, pulling back the curtains a little.

"Doesn't it seem like it just keeps snowing harder? It's class, don't you think?"

"I have to be in Barcelona tomorrow no later than ten."

I put the snow globe down on the bedside table, and before the snowman could challenge me with a look again, or the word "class" could make me back out of the whole thing, I went over to Pep and bit his lower lip. He tactfully pulled away and put his index finger to my mouth, tracing its outline.

"I don't only make tables and chairs."

"What?" I asked, puzzled.

"I work with an architect who makes sustainable homes. I create the wooden structures."

I nodded vaguely and my eyes begged him to shut up and get this going.

We took off our clothes quickly, our breathing out of sync, his desirous of me, mine angry with Mauro and the two boxes, mad at death and the damn cancelled flight. I tried not to look too closely at the strange new body. I couldn't help but compare, and it was odious to tell myself that I'd done well, that I'd found a much stronger, more powerful man who seemed totally comfortable with his nakedness, proud of his body, even. I ran my hands along his gym-sculpted curves and was surprised to find myself enjoying something I'd always considered superficial and secondary. He'd dumped me and then, insult to injury, he had died. Of course I deserved to lick some bronzer skin, play with a naughtier tongue, discover a more robust member. And the more I thought about how it had only been four weeks since all that horror, the more the calendar clung to my skin, the more I shivered, the more I got turned on. I didn't even pause to decipher the tattoo on his right bicep, or to consider whether I liked that his torso was waxed. I noticed Pep's visible erection and that was when I gave myself permission to let go. It was a prize, a living body, and I thought how I deserved it, even in my state of rage.

Sex between bonobos is unbridled. It usually lasts about ten seconds. Sex allows bonobos to walk a mile in each other's shoes. They aren't driven by orgasm or a search for release, sometimes it doesn't even have to do with reproduction. Bonobo sex is casual, easy, like any other social interaction. Sex replaces aggression, promotes communication, and functions as a means to reduce tension or resolve conflicts.

"What are you thinking about, Paula who doesn't look like a Paula?"

We were lying on top of the duvet, our hair messy, gazing

off into the distance, and he stroked my cheek with one finger.

"Nothing."

Inside we breathed in the sickly air of the room, while outside it continued to snow.

* * * * * *

Humour inhabits even the gloomy world of funerals. How else can you face a catalogue of urns that includes a biodegradable option for those who love to buy organic?

Before choosing the urn, we had been offered normal ashes, or snow-textured. I went with your sister. You know I never really could stand her. She's a more sophisticated version of your saintly mother. But she asked me to go with her and I went with her. I knew she didn't need me there, she's always been such a pragmatist. I went with her because I still love you. They asked us which ash texture we'd prefer and all I could do was smile. It was a reflex, an error of the nervous system. Really I was pure anguish, even now when I think about it, but I let out a laugh. Your sister looked at me, disconcerted. I asked what the difference was between the two options, and before the man dressed in grey formality could answer, I waved my hand to say never mind. Normal ash, I decided.

Days later, after smelling the penetrating odour of human ash—your ashes—I was glad I hadn't chosen the snow format. That way snow will always be the taste of pure, frozen water inside your mouth, do you remember it, too? Once, on an Easter week trip, you kissed me with your mouth filled with snow near the waterfall at Saut deth Pish and two days later you came down with a sore throat. I got really cross, I can't remember why. We had some place to go and we couldn't because you were in bed with a fever. Sometimes I was unfair to you in a cruel, deliberate way. I don't know why, I guess the protracted concessions of years of living together bring out the worst in us.

Snow-textured. Why do they insist on embellishing something as ugly as death?

* * * * * *

6

When I try to break it all down, I get stuck in a loop, revisiting facts I've gone over in my mind so many times, like someone returning obsessively to stare at a police report. Police reports have to describe the events in a strict sequence, without a single omission. Gaps are the worst. It's the gaps that rob me of my sleep in the early hours of the morning, and hold it hostage to my imaginings.

A report also has to be impartial: white woman, forty-two years old, resident of Barcelona, with no prior convictions, peels an orange in the silence of an immaculate kitchen, making sure the curl of rind doesn't break. Her father always does it that way too. When she was little he would tell her that if the curl broke she would never marry and inside she thought that, if she kept the curl unbroken, her mother would come back. Her gaze placed on no spot in particular, she is now an adult and knows that at best an orange will give her some vitamin C. She moves the citrus segments from one side of her mouth to the other and wonders if it makes sense now to have such a big dishwasher. She wonders, in fact, if it makes sense to have a dishwasher. She also wonders whether her hunger will ever again fill the dimensions of her kitchen. As she wonders, she is unaware that the man she ate lunch with a few hours earlier—who'd just announced I'm very

67

sorry but we need to talk, Paula, things haven't been working between us for a while now, there's someone else and I'm leaving, that man she looked at with fevered surprise—is expiring in a hospital.

The phone rings.

Her jacket hangs in the hallway.

It's February in Barcelona.

The cold and damp turn her fingers yellowish.

Afternoon rush hour.

Taxi. Yellow again, and black from now on.

Two bullets shot out, one after the other: his death and his duplicity. I feel I'm still carrying them inside me, with a pain that transforms Mauro into a saint or a traitor depending on which hits me harder.

My phone rang inside my bag and I assumed it was him. It had only been a couple of hours since we'd parted angrily. I let it ring as I ate the orange, restive. Its juice ran down my wrist. At the restaurant by the beach where he'd delivered all that unpleasantness, my mouth had turned dry, rough as my surprise. Living in a city by the sea usually adds a dramatic beauty to whatever tragedies happen there, but as he spoke, putting one cliché after the other, the sea did nothing, it didn't stir. The waves kept returning to the shore, like a wavy white summer skirt over tanned legs. Impassive, sterile beauty, refusing to darken in solidarity. The orange's vibrant, acid tang helped me organize my thoughts. The phone was ringing and I was thinking I'd tell him to cut it out, to stop insisting, that it was already too late. The ringing was so shrill that at moments I'm convinced that deep down I already knew that, when I answered, someone on the other end of the line would tell me that Mauro was dead. As if I was the one who had plotted his end. As if all that hate and rage parching my mouth had killed him.

I rolled my eyes, tired of the ringing, and sighed loudly as I rummaged through my bag looking for my mobile. I was surprised to see Nacho's name on the screen, and I cursed Mauro's cowardice, convinced he'd enlisted his best friend to persuade me that he meant me no harm. I thought, we're both adults, you git, how dare you use your friend to do your dirty work? And finally, in a fit of rage, I answered. I can't remember my life with Mauro without Nacho in the mix. He was a part of our everyday existence, with his outgoing personality and constant sarcasm. He and I had grown close over the years, and I appreciated his deep friendship with Mauro. Nacho was like a fixture in our home, in our life. Together he and Mauro owned a small publishing house that was finally turning a profit, but their friendship went much further back, from when they were boys who couldn't imagine they'd ever become men. Nacho's wife and I found ourselves pushed into a relationship because the four of us so often went out for dinner, and got together on weekends. She made me a little uncomfortable. It's not easy for me to meet new people outside my own circle, and I only very rarely feel a connection that can match what I have with my co-workers at the hospital. We spend so much time together, and our crushing defeats and crucial victories make us allies who share a unique language.

I never knew how to act around Nacho's wife, or what to talk to her about. Montse was anxious to be a mother, in a way I found overwhelming. She would explain in detail every aspect of her attempts to get pregnant when I didn't think we were that close. I didn't want to know what days she was ovulating. Mauro hoped I'd get on better with Montse, but I always felt that forcing a friendship was hypocritical and I never put in the effort. I liked Nacho and I didn't see why I had to include his wife in the same pack. Then they had the twins, so our double dates gradually became less frequent. I preferred it that way, I didn't need any awestruck woman explaining her breastfeeding to me as if it were some unique experience, forgetting that I work in a neonatology unit. I enjoyed Nacho more when he wasn't a Siamese twin. I wanted him as an individual, wandering around the house, beer in hand, brightening our routine. I would hunt out wheat beers, dark beers and other fancy kinds, Belgian beers, highest ABV, Scottish, and brandish barley and hops like crown jewels so he would extol my virtues in front of Mauro, slyly saying that I was a queen among women and that Mauro didn't deserve me. I liked to think that I made Mauro proud when I took such good care of his friend.

"Paula? Finally!"

"I don't want to hear it, Nacho, really. You can tell him to stop making a fool of himself like this… I don't want to hear from him."

"Paula, Mauro had an accident. A car... his bicycle. You have to come to the Clínic right now. Take a cab. He's going into surgery in ten minutes. I'll wait for you in the lobby at the Villarroel entrance."

"What are you talking about? Come on, he's already told me everything, we had lunch a little while ago," I said, following a speech I'd quickly memorized, blithe because I hadn't understood a single one of his words.

"Paula, Mauro's been in an accident. Come immediately!"

He hung up first. Then I followed suit, alarmed, and peeved with Nacho because he'd yelled and dropped all that information on me at once. When I explain to the parents of a premature baby that things aren't going well, I measure the information out with an eyedropper. You can't just vomit out bad news. After all, the message is still the same, but you have to mete out the information so it can be assimilated. I was thinking how later I would tell him off, tell him to never do that to me again.

In my hurry, I left the house without my jacket. When the February cold slapped me in the face, I turned around and went back upstairs, incongruent words dancing inside me: *accident, taxi, Mauro, bicycle, surgery, come, immediately*. I grabbed it from the coat rack in the hallway and spun back out the door. I didn't want to wait for the lift and I rushed down the three flights of stairs, the binary clack of my heels marking a rhythm befitting a military parade.

The race against the clock had begun. Countless times I've calculated the minutes I lost by forgetting my jacket.

71

During the first week after his death, I repeated the scene several times with my phone set to stopwatch. It was always two minutes, six seconds, and the fractions of a second varied according to how much I fumbled getting the keys into the lock. My father was appalled and said I should stop, but timing it helped me. Unlike everything else, there was a point to the timing. It had a justification, an objective; it had a methodology, a working plan I could use to make myself feel guilty; timing kept me linked to the moment before the cataclysm. I wanted that moment. I wanted to go back to it. I wanted to stay in it. There, by the sea, even as his ex. At least I'd be the ex of a living man. I couldn't think of any other way to turn back time.

The main description of a police report must be complete. It was Wednesday and children were leaving school, shouting with joy in a way that terrified me. The children were leaving school and their parents, oblivious to my suffering, were picking them up at the different centres scattered across the city, double-parking oversized cars, or up on the sidewalk with their hazards on, making my cabbie grumble and curse them all, complicating traffic that was already hostile to begin with. Children were leaving school, surrounded by the smell of salami, cologne and tangerines just as a cloud-covered sun started to set over Barcelona, just as Mauro was putting the finishing touches to the portrait of his life: intracranial pressure elevated by trauma, coma, cardiac arrest. There was no need to bring him into surgery.

—

We humans are always giving ourselves marks, from birth to death. We rank the knowledge we acquire, the arses we caress, the homes we inhabit, and the countries we visit. We need to grade things. A death soon after an accident, during the initial evaluation of a polytraumatic patient, is called a "second peak" mortality, and represents thirty per cent of deaths. That morning I had rated a baby at above eight on the Apgar scale, a healthy, plump child with a full head of hair; that same afternoon, in another hospital, a doctor with a bushy moustache hiding a comical mouth that didn't seem proper for delivering such grim news marked Mauro as a five in the head and neck, abdomen, lumbar spine and pelvic contents. A five, in that marking system, represents a critical situation, uncertain survival.

But by the time I got there, it was absolutely certain: he was dead.

"Everything happened very quickly," the doctor informed us. Nacho took my hand and squeezed it very hard. And, as if it were the chorus of a song we knew by heart, we waited for the second part of the refrain. "We did everything we could. I'm so sorry."

They had said goodbye in front of the publishing house. As I listened to the story, attentive for a moment where I could still change something, Nacho's right leg was moving nonstop, shaking the entire row of chairs in the waiting room where we sat. Nacho turned to go back into the office while Mauro put on his helmet. He rang the bell on his bike to say goodbye to his friend and business partner, who was now speaking to me with wide eyes as he sipped from a small plastic cup someone had given us at some point. Dry mouth as prelude to a damp fear filling the diaphragm with a disconsolate puddle.

Nacho turned to wave at him. He says he smiled. A few seconds later, before the door had closed behind him, he heard the crunch. The car appeared on the left. It had run a red light. Nacho chose certain phrases to explain what happened and I've accepted them as final. I recorded them inside me with a precise narrative rhythm, but there are gaps, and they are perverse. Sometimes when I can't sleep I recreate the scene over and over again to fill them in. My scientific side needs to know everything, carry out an exploratory study. I focus on the ordinary circumstances in which the accident took place, I need to know if there were other people around, what they were doing, what they did when the bicycle was on the ground, know if he'd told Nacho that I knew, if they'd talked about when he was planning to move out, if he'd explained that I'd refused to hug him, there by the sea when he was trying to calm me down. I need to imagine the sounds on the street in that moment because all I have are the bike's bell and the crunch. Nacho didn't mention any other sounds. In my mind I keep replaying Mauro's smile, that fateful crunch and finally the fear in his pupils, behind the insufficient protection of his glasses.

There in the waiting room that had already become a funerary chapel, I couldn't take my eyes off a tiny stain on Nacho's shirt, a stain that was like a door opening onto the horror, a tiny dark red spot, the unmistakable red of deoxidized blood. The door opened wide. Mauro's parents and sister arrived and we hugged each other without thinking twice. Our heads were nearly touching, we formed a circle tied up with arms. Sobbing bodies, flagging legs and abstracted thoughts; I propped them all up with my distance and incredulity, more able to focus on the irritating perfume that the woman who had effectively been my mother-in-law was wearing than on grasping that they were mourning the death of a son, of a brother. In that moment, family bonds took on crucial importance. Mother, father, sister. The family tree revealed itself to me with all its branches. Family of Mauro Sanz? And Nacho and I, still alone in the waiting room, had stood up automatically, coordinated in a choreography of fear. But now the limbs of the tree had arrived, cracked by a pain that couldn't be like mine. A father's pain is different from a mother's and a mother's is different from a sister's, and a woman's pain is different from that of a woman who's just been dumped.

Something was distancing me from reality, there was so much hardness that I was unable to cry, unable to make the breathy whistling wounded-animal sound that Mauro's mother was making, or weep with his father's inconsolable, deep sobbing. That distant professor, with a PhD in Geography and Spatial Planning, who never uttered more than a couple of words, was now bawling with no filter. I couldn't take it much longer, there was no escape from those desperate fingers digging into my shoulders like claws and somehow forcing me to be part of a family. They welcomed me in their loss and presented me with a starring role that in the coming months would take on a weight I was not yet able to calculate. Those decisions that we cannot take for ourselves are the ones that interrogate who we are and who we are becoming.

The forty-two-year-old white woman, resident of Barcelona and with no police record, doesn't cry, doesn't speak, doesn't think clearly, and sees a young woman entering the waiting room. At this point she only realizes that the woman is tall and thin and walks with the elegance of a ballerina. From that point on, she calls her "the ballerina". Still a prudent distance away from all of us, the ballerina turns her head in every direction as if hearing her name called from different angles. The white woman who doesn't cry, doesn't speak, doesn't think clearly sees how the ballerina's beauty contrasts with the frozen defeat written on our faces, all of us trapped in that room, and most of all the ballerina spatters us with her shocking youthful freshness. She is filled with light. Long, thin, vibrant black hair with no sign of dye or fake colours. Her features in their right place. Her skin, enviable. Nothing wrinkled, or falling, no mark of time; clean, she gives off a delightful glow. The ballerina walks here and there, covering her mouth with a trembling hand, as if she were looking for someone. Her other hand tightly grips the handle of a leather bag hanging from her shoulder. The ballerina begins to conform to the atmosphere of nervousness and desperation in that waiting room. And then Nacho calls out to her.

"Carla!"

Nacho got up and went over to her. He placed both hands on her shoulders and said something. The only thing he could say. She folded onto her knees, like rubber, and dropped her bag to the floor. Nacho lifted her up and walked her over to the row of chairs. We sat beside each other. She was pale and her lips were practically white. With a voice that sounded older than she looked, she kept repeating: "No, you're lying. Tell me he's not dead. It's a lie, you're lying." She seemed very vulnerable. Something prompted me to run an arm over her shoulder and offer her some water. It wasn't me, it was a veneer I'm able to don because of my profession.

"Paula, this is Carla," said Nacho, despondent. I stared at him in an attempt to let him know that he had failed me as a friend and he avoided my eyes.

Carla. The power of a name. Carla is a place, a fact, a suspicious perfume, a story, a bitter memory, hoarse laughter, a suspicion that may always have been there. Carla is a hidden world.

She lifted her head quickly and cut off that litany of truth and lies. It was obvious, from the immediacy of her reaction, that my name meant something to her, she placed me somehow. She scrutinized me with weepy eyes the colour of almonds, and swallowed hard. She still had saliva in her mouth. I tried to remain in my professional role, which protected me like a breastplate. In the empathic, compassionate tone I've learnt to use when speaking to parents racked with pain, carefully choosing the first words to break the hostile silence of preparing for the worst, I asked her if she wanted to call someone. I needed to make clear that Mauro had always had a strong woman by his side, someone capable of controlling a situation like that and not getting unnerved by her presence. He was the one I wanted to shout and spit at, but you can't blame a dead man: "You see how I wasn't crazy? You see how there was something wrong between us?" The thought of another woman had crossed my mind many times, but I was convinced that accusing him of such a worn-out cliché would make me look petty and vulnerable.

And she started up again with it can't be true, covering her face with her hands, fidgeted, it seemed she'd lost interest in me, there was now no point in her knowing anything about me. I felt ridiculous.

All of a sudden, I realized the magnitude of what had just happened. Mauro was gone forever.

I waited in the hospital lobby, over hazy, fathomless hours, lost somewhere between sleep and waking, greeting family members who arrived shocked, and repeating the same story again and again. Those same words would continue to hit my flesh like shrapnel even days later, in other airless moments: his wake, his funeral.

The bicycle.

The red light.

Forty-three years old.

It can't be. I still can't believe it, Paula.

A tragedy.

Haven't seen you in so long, Paula.

May his memory be a blessing, Paula.

My God, Paula, I'm so sorry.

You have to take care of yourself, you hear me?

Some of them cried as they offered me their condolences. They offered them to me. Where was the ballerina?

A police report must be easily understood. It continues with the appearance of Mauro's sister in the lobby, a crumpled tissue in her hand, her eyes swollen and small, her nose red, her expression exuding nervous exhaustion. For a few days we all looked like that; I even felt my muscles were flaccid. The white woman, forty-two years old, resident of Barcelona and with no priors, wants nothing to do with her but was raised by her father to keep certain emotions at bay and hold back certain cathartic remarks; he had a piano to vent on, she didn't, so she stifles it the way only she knows how.

"I'll call you tomorrow, Paula, when I'm feeling a little more composed, if you don't mind."

"…"

"Do you know, did he ever mention whether he wanted to be buried or cremated…? He never talked to us about any of that."

The white woman is devastated by the sister's verb tense. By degrees, Mauro is becoming part of the past.

"Isn't it too soon?" asks the white woman in a thin voice.

"What do you mean?"

79

But she doesn't know how to answer. Too soon to give him up for dead, too soon to have to think about the funeral. Too soon to have to believe it.

From that night on the flat fills with a shadow, a heavy thing that comes into the house with me, sticks to the furniture, to the walls, to the fabric on the sofa. It impregnates the doorknobs, the ceramic bowl in the hallway, the clothes, the sheets, the toothbrush. It clings to my expressions, to my face in the mirror, to the coffeepot, to the distant voice of the TV news anchor, to the telephone that won't stop ringing. For a couple of days Mauro's sister is a scab on burnt skin. She makes the heavy shadow grow and gives it monstrous form, filling the flat with words like *death notice, morgue, urn, wreath, coffin, flowers*. The flowers. The plants. The flowers. Mauro. I gazed out, onto the terrace, but she pulled me back to the catalogues and the funeral paperwork that insisted on beautifying life's failure so we could look it in the face again, and perhaps some day make peace with it.

"Really, Paula. Don't you remember ever having talked with him about the kind of interment he wanted?"

I shrugged and chewed on the inside of my cheek. I wanted her out of the house, I wanted to pummel her. The word *interment* seemed archaic and out of place. We'd talked about cars, trips, we'd discussed children we would never have, we had talked about what he'd look like bald and me with grey hair, I had shouted at him that there was no worse trap between two people than a mortgage, we had laughed as we swore we'd never retire. That was as far as we'd got with projecting our futures, but no, about interments, about what sort we'd each like, we hadn't ever talked about that.

"Ashes," I exclaimed to cut the conversation short. "We had a favourite cove. Let's do ashes, please."

Close off the horror.

Abbreviate it with rituals.

Shed the mortuary vocabulary.

Shed the corpse.

Get angry with him for lying.

Grieve all the rest of him.

All the rest that was no longer salvageable.

Leaving my jacket and going back for it robbed me of two minutes, seven seconds and some vague fractions, all those kids laughing and shouting and blocking my way as they got into cars and their mothers put their seat belts on, said see you tomorrow. For them there was a seat belt. For them there was a tomorrow.

I should have been able to get there when he was still alive, to scream his name, and since there was no brain death, his brain would have been able to create a final image of me, of me by his side. I should have been faster.

Two minutes, seven seconds, and some vague fractions of a second. You forget your jacket and the tragedy becomes abusive, gargantuan, and all of a sudden its disproportionate enormity has nothing to do with the drama of the accident, or even with death itself. You forget a jacket and the dispro-portionate enormity is in the fact that you weren't by his side, to comfort him. I wasn't by his side to hold him, and I wasn't able to forgive him.

* * * * * *

Since you've been gone, all I expect from the telephone
are offers to change service providers, and tragedies. The
ring still scares me every time. I'm shrouded in that *still*.
Still scares me, I still wake up gasping for breath, I still turn
every time I pass a bicycle. Without thinking, I still set the
table for two on Friday evenings. When I do crossword
puzzles I still reach for your hand on the sofa and ask you:
"Six letters, to rain in fine drops." I still sigh when I get
no response. I still reread the text that says, "I would run
away with you if I could, Carla." I still look at the video of
her blowing you a kiss from a rubber dinghy about to go
down some rapids, dressed in neoprene, wearing a life vest
and helmet, laughing and splashing the screen. I still blush
when my name pops up as an annoyance in your chats. And
now, when I answer the phone, after the shock of the first
ring, if they're calling from the bank asking for you or for
the head of the household, you know what, Mauro? Now
I enjoy saying out loud that you aren't here, and I so hope
that they'll insist a little more, that they'll ask when is a good
time to reach you, so I can tell them that you won't be home,
that you're dead. Now I enjoy giving them that small shock
and I chafe against their condolences when they say, "I'm
so sorry, ma'am. Forgive me." And I hang up and there's

the void again. And I still charge your mobile and leave it at a hundred per cent battery and then wait for it to get all used up, as if you were real and those trivial things were keeping you alive.

* * * * * *

7

"They could turn ice into water and make clouds in a laboratory, isn't that right, Paula?"

Martina is peeling a chestnut with her little fingers and has been deliberating on how to bring rain to drought-stricken areas. She is a small replica of her mother, the way she moves and her blue eyes, the way she speaks, the image she projects, of a tyrant with Lilliputian features and the world at her feet, and, just like her mother, her sweetness and grace overpower and conquer her subjects. I'm afraid I'm the only one who's paying attention to her game. I don't know much about how to deal with kids her age, I like them better when they barely weigh anything and are struggling to find their way in the world. I tend to think that happy children, old enough to talk, walk and eat on their own, don't need me. Often though, when I'm with Lídia's daughters, I feel that they're supplying me with a dose of innocence and gratuitous happiness and that, possibly, there's no simpler, more effective remedy for a self-absorbed adult than getting swept up in a child's chitchat. Her sister, who in little more than a year has become a tetchy hormone hidden behind a fringe and in constant communion with a mobile phone, sits awkwardly on spindly legs. She's been ignoring us from across the table, texting as if the world were ending, and the girls' father, who a moment earlier was dragging out the final syllables of his words as he tried to converse with me about the upcoming American elections, is now sleeping on the sofa, his head back and his mouth open, with crumbs of marzipan on his chest. I would brush them off, but I'm afraid to wake him and besides, it's fun to see him looking so ridiculous, something he'd never allow if he were awake.

I do my best not to show how sleepy the meal has made me and, as always happens when I visit this house, my eyes are drawn to a photograph that lives on the table by the TV alongside a few others. It's Lídia and me in the Atacama Desert and we must have been barely twenty. Our skin and hair are toasted by the sun and the gratification of starting out on our adult lives, the first powerful whiff of freedom. We met in our first year of med school, shortly before that unforgettable trip. I was captivated by her ability to take the lead. A week after classes started she had already volunteered to be the student liaison and set up study groups for anyone interested, and she treated the professors with the confidence of someone who'd spent half their life at university. She was a first-year medical student, like me, but my nerves and shyness amid all the new faces was the polar opposite of her ease and self-assurance. Petite and athletic, she had naturally impeccable style; I envied the way she carried herself, and her slight insolence when presenting her arguments, sometimes even getting professors up against the ropes.

We barely spoke the first semester, even though I'd been watching her; I didn't think I could just approach someone as popular as she was without a good reason. We didn't talk until the day she asked to borrow my notes from cellular bio because she'd missed the previous class.

"What does this say?" She pointed at my notes with a confused expression.

"I'm sorry, he was talking so fast I had trouble getting it all down."

"And you've already got doctor's handwriting. This could be Sanskrit, or Cyrillic." She laughed loudly. Her incisors are a tad separated, giving her a slightly mischievous quality.

I had the feeling that her energy was different from mine, you could see it in her powerful way of speaking. Effusive and witty, she seemed so sure of herself. I kept everything in, studied each word before saying it, just as I'd been studying her since day one. I envied her clothes, her casual familiarity that drew people to her, circles of students forming around her, I envied her strength and the way she held her chin, that invincible aura surrounding her.

For a few seconds we looked at each other in recognition, and I was aware that something durable was being born in that encounter between long-suffering and prudent me and this carefree, extroverted creature. Over time, we learnt that, through osmosis, we balanced each other out: what one lacked, the other had in abundance. Her characteristic authority had lessened over the years, and even though it's not nice to say, our need to get together often and talk every day the way we used to had also waned. Her life choices, with husband and daughters, schedules and schools, was hard to match with mine, which was much more pared down, but since Mauro's been gone we've felt that same mutual emotional need we had in the beginning; she needs to let me know that she's there for me, more for herself, I think, than for me. I don't hold that against her, I'm used to her putting herself at the centre, and it does me good to let out all my feelings at her insistence, and finally I tell her that if it weren't for a red light Mauro would have left me.

I get distracted trying to calculate how long I've known her. My addition and subtraction are hampered by the sweet Muscat wine that's clouded my head, but I smile with my eyes at little Martina so she won't doubt I'm fascinated by her talk of artificial rain.

Inside myself, I'm focused on the years, recounting with an imaginary abacus. The arithmetic that traces out a life in easy strokes: university, her wedding, her hospital placement, mine, the year Mauro and I met. Lídia's first pregnancy, our both specializing in paediatrics, the trips, the friends, getting placed at the same hospital, the flat, neonatology, her second pregnancy, and when the list sinks in, I leap out of my chair.

I find Lídia alone in the kitchen with the murmur of the dishwasher in the background, clearing up the last of the meal. Her curls gambol as she ferries around the dishes and puts everything away in Tupperware. She's a Tupperware lady, she has all the sizes and colours and considers them among her prized possessions. It doesn't match with my memory of the most popular woman in the department, but here she is, breaking the mould, surrounded by plastic containers.

"You know what, Lídia?" I enter the kitchen.

"The girls are fighting and Toni's snoring on the couch, right?"

"Do you know how long we've known each other?"

"What?"

"We've known each other for twenty-five years!"

"Twenty-five? Are we that old?"

I'm surprised to see her drop her gaze into the sink and slow her activity, surprised that it reminds her of time's passage instead of the cause for celebration that made me leap up from my chair.

"We should celebrate, don't you think?"

I bump her with my hip and throw up my hands, pretending to shake some invisible maracas, but I realize she isn't sharing my joy.

"Do you know what day it is today, Paula?"

"I know perfectly well. Don't even think about mentioning what day it is today. Twenty-five years, Lídia! Don't you think it's a good reason to go out for a drink?"

She grabs a tea towel and dries her hands, turns towards me, pushes a curl from her face.

"Paula... I don't want to overstep the mark, but I don't think pretending that today is just another day is helping you."

The good mood vanishes. Her words stick in my heart like a damp gust off the cemetery walls. A day devoted to remembering the dead, as if we didn't remember the dead every day. November first. First thing in the morning. The first and only message on my machine:

"Paula, good morning, sweetheart. Today will be a rough day for you. I'm going to take flowers to your mother, if you want to come. It might rain so I'm going to take a cab to Montjuïc. I thought we could go together this year. Let me know so I can firm up my plans, OK?"

The beep of the machine.

"There are no more messages." There never are.

I've been sitting on the floor for a while now, tracing a little slit between two strips of parquet, pretending I know nothing about the ashy cumulonimbus trying to swallow up the normality I'd imposed on myself today. I rehearsed how to tell my father that today marked nine months filled with rough days, and that it's been thirty-five years since Mum's been gone, so that's twelve thousand seven hundred and seventy-five rough days, twelve thousand seven hundred and seventy-five days of looking at a black-and-white photograph on the bedside table. A span of time long enough for you to have grasped that your daughter doesn't need to wait for a specific day of the year to remember those who are no longer around, and who—like Mauro's ashes—are here and there and everywhere. I didn't miss anything today at Montjuïc. I finally called my father back, but all I said was, you go ahead, I'm feeling poorly, body aches, coming down with a flu, thanks for the invitation. Spontaneous white lies, after sensing the strangeness and knowing I have to protect myself, as always, unable to explain to anyone this strangeness that no one else notices, not even Lídia, not even my father. It's unsettling when two previously isolated events, my mother's death—which I'd got past and shelved somewhere distant inside my childhood head—and Mauro's death—tumultuous and still alive inside this new head of mine—are suddenly connected, and totalled up together, and the world convulses.

The cumulonimbus has a wide, dark base and climbs to a great height. That allows me to glance at the stage where it seems my life will play out from now on, and I hate not finding any traces of what it used to be until recently. Until not long ago at all. Nine months isn't that long. It's enough to give shape to a life in utero and enough to remember a death.

All Saints' Day.

The Day of the Dead.

Mum.

Mauro.

The days grow shorter and nature enters into a state of apparent death. Where is the sea, the salt, the watermelon? Where are the smiles, where is the light?

"I'll go with you if you want."

"Go with me where?"

"Where do you think, Paula? To the cemetery. I'll leave the girls with Toni and we'll be there in a second. Do you want to bring flowers?"

"Do you want to shut up?"

She takes my hand before I can leave the kitchen and hugs me. I resist, get angry. Pull away.

"Good thing we didn't know each other at seven when my mother died, Lídia, because I swear I wouldn't have been able to put up with you for more than five minutes. Why do you always make such a big deal about things?"

The shadow unfolds, efficiently, and falls on my friend. Despite it all, I feel satisfied at having finally spat out something tangible, something that helps me understand what's going on.

The battle is won, for the time being, by the gloomy spirit that won't allow me to apologize. Not yet. For months I've had the enigmatic taste of bitterness in my mouth, let Lídia have it too, with her whole, uncracked life, with her pretty, healthy daughters and her solutions for everything, with her Tupperware and her balanced menus, a husband who falls asleep on the couch in front of me unapologetically and her excessive determination to celebrate Christian rituals, or Celtic, or wherever this holiday comes from. A life without deaths. Here, Lídia, have a little grief. My gift to you, try it.

"I'm not making a big deal of it, Paula. But you're acting like nothing's going on and I'm worried you'll suddenly realize and explode, and then it'll all be a lot worse."

Some pink spots blaze on her neck and face, like panicked lights flickering, but how could she possibly quantify my pain? She has no idea of how all proportion flies out the window, how grief can no longer be measured on a human scale, instead calculated now in concrete acts: lingering on the sofa until late into the night to avoid getting into an empty bed. Hearing new songs on the radio on the way to work and thinking how Mauro will never get that chance, sleeping clutching the green pullover he bought in Reykjavik, using the last few grams of toasted sesame seeds we'd bought together, and remembering how we'd laughed when we unrolled the newspaper cone they came in and saw that it was a page of dating adverts. Every act has a size, a height and a weight, and their total is the measurement of the emptiness and pain I feel when I try to accept that I no longer was part of his plans for the future.

Deep down I sense that Lídia is right, that everything could be much worse and I don't know it yet. I almost need a miracle to unravel the knot where the shadow has us trapped, but maybe that's what friendship is, the miracle that alleviates everything, that disarms me because it's a familiar place and I urgently, increasingly urgently, need signs of normality.

"I didn't mean to say what I said. I wish I'd known you when I was seven years old, you hear me? I'll go tomorrow, or some other day. Or maybe I won't, Lídia. I just don't like cemeteries. Who likes going to the cemetery? What do you do in a cemetery?"

"But that's why I said it. At least today there'll be people, and flowers and colours. I'll drive you there. It's good to remember him today."

"I don't like remembering him there." And I implore her with my eyes to confirm that my mother and Mauro are somewhere else, somewhere without plaques engraved

93

with their names and a niche number, far from materials designed to withstand the inclement weather of the great beyond.

The ashes divided in grams, transferred into two plastic bags. My bag decanted into a biodegradable urn so I can let it float illegally out into the sea. The other bag to the cemetery on Montjuïc, inside a niche, obeying his mother's orders to the last. Such an emphatically painstaking man, now scattered in a grey mess for the rest of eternity.

Martina comes through the kitchen door eagerly. She's hiding something in her little fists and struggles to make her way over to show it to us.

"Look, look!" Her shrill, eager tone forces me to wipe away a treacherous tear with the cuff of my jumper.

Martina opens her hands and tosses up a pile of tiny bits of aluminium foil she's carefully cut.

"I figured out how to make rain!"

I look up and will myself to believe I'm five years old. Babies don't shed tears until four to six weeks after birth. Crying doesn't actually have a concrete physiological function, it's a side effect of stimulating the nervous system. I struggle to control them. I order myself to stop and I stop.

The silvery bits fall in slow motion and cover all of Barcelona with a purifying rain, including the cemetery to the southeast with its hundreds of thousands of graves, one of which is my mother Anna's, with its aged marble covered by yellow flowers—cheery and alive—that my father must have brought her today. Another grave is new, recent, the cement sealing it still tender. Carla must have brought him a white flower or two because, face it, Paula, he belonged to her a little too.

8

The days pass, colourless and identical, onerous in a way that's hard to pinpoint. I work a lot, sleep little, eat even less and remember too much. Technically there's nothing I can do. I've lost control over myself.

After my shifts I go running along the Aigües road, trying to exhaust myself in the hopes of being able to sleep at some point. There's a professor at the University of Texas, a psychologist who studies the impact of sleep deprivation, which they call "white torture". He explains how someone who doesn't sleep over an extended period of time usually becomes psychotic, starts to hallucinate and experiences interruptions to their basic cognitive functions. White torture leaves no physical marks and as such is harder to prove in front of a judge. I refuse to ask Santi for a few days off to rest. If you look at it that way, I'm my own torturer, and in my own custody. Punishment, interrogation, dissuasion. Who knows what my objective is. So I run. I run focusing on my breathing, on the minutes, on the seconds, on my heart beating, I run and flee myself.

No matter how early I get out, there are always other people and that's why I like it. The feeling of absence has started to be exhausting. This morning I stopped at the foot of the Fabra observatory, panting, in an empty spot. It smelt of moss and damp life. I closed my eyes to feel safe. The muffled autumn sun warmed my face and was so pleasant I felt I had to hold on to the moment. Two birds splashed in a puddle. When my mother fell sick and we lost her a few months later, my father became a diehard birdwatcher. He would obsessively fill his weekends with trips and hikes and I would follow along, dragging my feet, with no choice in the matter, as penance, binoculars hanging around my neck and those two off-kilter bunches that neither of us knew how to comb properly. He volunteered with banding networks, marked the birds, calculated their survival rates and measured their reproductive success on some yellow cards he lugged up and down with a passion that bordered on the fanatical. When he had ringed more than five hundred individual birds of fifty different species, he earned the title of expert ringer. Meanwhile, I watched him and wished that he would take me in his hands with the same care, that he would place a numbered metal ring around my ankle and give me the opportunity to offer him precise information on my age and my yearning to migrate back to when we'd been a family of three, not so very long before.

He gave me bird posters that meant nothing to me. As I got older, while my friends' bedroom walls were covered with the latest pop stars, mine had one poster of the swallows and swifts that nest in Catalonia, another with five rows of Amazon parrots in varying shades of green, and yet another featuring the brown and ochre tones of Iberian birds of prey. My father believes that birds are intelligent creatures, that some species are so intelligent as to rival primates and even humans. It's still a recurring subject in his conversations, which I avoid because all I have to say about birds is that, in my experience, they were replacements for a wife. The invasion of the birds was how we contained the river's waters, kept from losing control, forgot the stifled sound of my father during those first nights without Mum, him sobbing over the piano, the sofa and the Berber kilim she'd bought second-hand in the south of France and absolutely loved. For my dad, the birds began as a retaining wall, then became a hobby, and then a nest of new friendships that made him smile, so I learnt not to question his method of handling his grief, even though it was sometimes very embarrassing for me, especially when he would quiz me on bird names in front of new people he wanted to impress. I understood that if I went along with it things would be easy, emotionally. My father is a practical man and, as for me, well, I figured that if there were species capable of retaining between two hundred to two thousand different songs in a brain a thousand times smaller than mine, I should be able to handle the infinite void left by my mother somehow. I went on more hikes than any other child my age and I let him cover my walls with birds until I moved out at twenty years old, never confessing that my fear of birds was off the charts. I was repelled by their abrupt head movements, their fragile legs like tiny branches, and the hot, trembling bodies beneath their feathers, quivering in my hands when he made me hold them so he could get their rings on.

Eventually I learnt them all by heart, even their scientific names, but over time I've let them fall by the wayside, as a defence mechanism. That morning I wasn't sure whether the birds in the puddle were siskins or serins. Seized by an attack of melancholy and without thinking it over, I snapped a photo with my phone and sent it to my father. He replied in less than two seconds. "Male siskin. Don't you see the top of his head is black? Are you coming for lunch on Sunday? Love you."

Lunch with Dad on Sunday. Again. Another Sunday. Forty-two years. I kick the ground hard to scare off the birds and angrily pull a branch off a bush without realizing it has thorns and, just my luck, one goes right into my fingertip. "Don't you see, Pauli? It's karma. That's what you get for being grumpy." I stop to think how that must be what people mean when they say they hear the dead. "Does it hurt? It's a *Rubus ulmifolius*, the thorns are horrible but in late August it'll have ripe blackberries. You could make jam, what do you say? You up for it?" But I'm sure it can't be so banal, hearing the dead must be more dramatic, with clouds parting like in a painting by Turner, and the leaves on the trees must shake like mad. Beethoven must be playing, at least. That's how it has to be, right? What I'm hearing now must just be me forcing the memory, me making copies of the original. Nothing more than that. I smile at the void, in resignation. After struggling with the thorn I finally manage to extract it with a few little squeezes. I look out at the blue line of the sea that always marks some hypothetical escape route.

I search there for consolation with the metallic taste of blood on my tongue, and soon begin stroking the body of my mobile phone with my frozen hands. My fingers move of their own volition, a step ahead of my brain, tired of so much equanimity. Unable to resist as they make their way to the phone's contacts. Once there, they scroll up and down, again and again, wandering from A to Z, from Z to A, finally stopping at P. Pep. I look back out at the sea and then around me. I can't help feeling a surge of shame. I don't know what to say to him. You can't just call someone after months of silence to ask them to come over and make love to you until you've calmed down and can fall asleep; nevertheless, I feel I could ask that of him and he'd accept, he would make it easy, accessible, there'd be no consequences or questions, just that sexual bond that may be what I need to get some sleep: human contact, being touched, being fondled, made to remember that I exist, someone taking their time undoing all the buttons that are stifling me, filling my house with sounds, a real, live man whispering into my ear and warming me with the hot breath of earthbound words. My fingers are anxious to push on his name; they dance restlessly on the mobile, aware they are playing with fire.

"Don't turn off the light, please, I want to look at you."

We were in another hotel, another neutral room, but he was inspecting every inch of my body with identical desire. I automatically repress the memory, erase the image of his hands deep in my flesh, the warmth of his skin, the slow fluttering of his eyelashes when he entered me rhythmically, and the timid laughter of us both when the bed creaked. But my fingers win out, going straight to his short, powerful name that now fills the centre of the screen. Pep. I feel a twinge in the small wound left by the thorn when I touch his name, a name that when you say it aloud sounds just like a prick to the finger. A short name for a man I sense won't last for very long. I bring the phone close to my ear, expectant. One ring, two rings, my heart beating so hard my T-shirt is trembling, three rings. It goes to voicemail and I hang up.

"Fuck it!"

I grab a handful of sand and throw it at nothing in particular, furious, cursing the stupid impulse to call him. Forget him, Paula.

Forgetting should come naturally. You should be able to forget in the very moment you decide to forget. Forgetting should be immediate, otherwise remembering becomes degrading, and at the same time an act of resistance. I don't want to forget him. I want to stop philosophizing and start tearing out my hair, I want to shatter a vase on the floor, hide under a pillow, I want someone besides my father to invite me to lunch. I want to live like I did before, splatter an occasional evening with the perfume of flirtation. That's all I want, the contradiction of feeling able to move forward just to recover everything I've left behind.

I spend the day waiting for the phone to ring and deploy a whole spectrum of excuses for his silence, possibilities that range from defeatist—he changed his number, his phone's broken, he doesn't have service—to more dramatic—that he doesn't want to have anything more to do with me, that something serious happened that's keeping him from calling me back, that he's dead. Why not? I straighten up, take a deep breath and accuse myself of being a drama queen, before berating myself for my new tendency to take everything to the worst-case scenario. I remind myself that everything is still in its place, the clouds, the sea, my insomnia, the dead. Nobody else died, Paula, and I set off on a run.

Dinner was soup from a packet, a glass of wine and an apple. A hostile choice. I should eat more, and better, skip those nasty soups, but I'm cold and I can do whatever I feel like because I'm a single woman coming home to an empty house. I don't have to set an example for kids, or force myself to make meals enjoyable. Total, absolute freedom to turn into a recluse. This is not the right attitude but there's no one around to tell me that. As my glass of wine empties and I refill it, I get the urge to call Pep again. I don't know if I should and my nervous hesitation feels pleasant, surprising. I immediately backpedal, reminding myself that he's probably seen my call from the morning by now, so his silence can only indicate I shouldn't insist. It's incongruous to feel pleasure over something negative, but I'm enjoying the layer of uncertainty—will he return my call?—over the same old soundtrack of every evening: the TV news and the coming and going of neighbours in the stairwell. Come on, Paula, you're forty-two years old. How can you be walking around with this childish expectation clinging to the walls of your stomach?

I hear the door to the street. It seems my hearing has sharpened lately; it's part of the expectant state I enter into as soon as I walk through the door of what is now my home. Only mine. As I pour myself a little more wine and check the mobile's screen for the umpteenth time, I hear Thomas coming into the building with someone else. It's her. I recognize the echo of her stilettos. Keys jingle throughout their conversation in English and their laughter, in no language. He introduced me to her a few days ago at the foot of the stairs. She's blonde and has a UV tan maintained twelve months a year. She had on black leather trousers. She's much older than Thomas, she must be fifty, but she keeps the years at bay with some very expensive techniques. She is preceded by a strong, sweet perfume that reels you into her net, but her eyes are vulnerable and her face is that of an innocent girl, shattering all the cougar clichés. I hear the door to Thomas's flat open and now comes the sound that will make my heart explode. The sound of a spontaneous kiss. Two mouths searching for and briefly greeting each other. The acoustics of the stairwell amplify the sound, making it echo, and it reaches my ear with all its choreography, two lips pressing together and separating with traction. I feel so empty, I miss that gesture so much I have to choke down my rage. White torture leaves no physical marks, just these owl eyes, a bowed head, and my heart in a fist over the sound of a kiss. I need to sleep. I need that damn kiss.

Pep won't call. I wipe off my make-up listlessly while I look at myself in the mirror. I'm pale, pale grey, like the grey faces of cloistered nuns with velvety skin covered in fine wrinkles. Is it just how I see myself or does everyone else see me this way too? Is it scientifically proven that if you add up a lack of sex, sleep and human contact with excessive doses of sadness, your skin changes colour?

I'll have to look for an article about that.

The light's gone out of my face.

My eyes are shrunken.

Are my friends noticing and commenting on my diminishing release of progesterone, endorphins and collagen?

Tomorrow I'm going to run an extra kilometre.

When you lose your spouse past a certain age, it's understood as a fact of life, a law of nature, and everyone grants you asylum under the protective blanket of grief. No one even thinks of meddling in your curtailed sexual activity and truncated love life; on the other hand, young people like me who've been left alone are trapped at an impasse outside space and time, locked in a cage with no identifying label, examined with a magnifying glass and bombarded with questions disguised as compassion. They are handed down a verdict of mandatory reconstruction: still young and fertile, they must find someone who will reactivate their desire, give them butterflies in their stomach again. They don't know how to respond, because there's no etiquette book with a chapter on death in spring, they keep quiet, unable to convey the feeling they've lost a part of their biography.

I get into bed but I'm not tired so I pick up the novel I've been reading. It's about an older widow who suggests to her neighbour, who's a widower, that they sleep in the same bed and keep each other company at night, so they can talk before going to sleep, feel that human warmth under the sheets, and nothing more. I've read less than a paragraph when I hear sounds from the flat upstairs. The noises started a few weeks ago. I can clearly distinguish the tanned blonde with the amiable gaze moaning in English. We moan in different languages, moans of pleasure aren't inarticulate sounds, they somehow echo your native language. Soon I realize I'm paying more attention to the sounds from the flat upstairs than is polite. I close the book. I feel a tickle between my legs, something vibrates inside me, activated by the damp rumpus going on upstairs. I try to keep reading but before long I hear the sounds of Thomas in ecstasy. I could cry with envy, like a little girl who wants what she can't have. I yearn to exist, to be a physical body and shed my skin like a snake, move forward and leave the dried-out casing of grief in the middle of the road. For a boy to find the dry mantle and lift it off the ground with a stick while admiring the snake that slithers anew, down the road, with gleaming skin and a lust for life. Finally I fall asleep with the book open over my face and a last thought that sounds like Mauro's voice beside me. "That book you're reading is crap, Paula. Pick up a Russian for once."

—

When dreams aren't revealing, they are merely the involution of our days. When they are, though, they can transform into a circus that sparks to life with a wide-eyed magic. Thomas's fingers play with my nipples, spinning them like a thief intent on finding the combination to a safe. I hear the sound of a telephone and I'm reluctant to disengage from the warmth of that oneiric choreography. I like feeling Thomas's hand on my skin. "It's fine, go on," I murmur. The phone rings at the end of a corridor as long as my dream is strange. I wake up suddenly, annoyed with myself and very ashamed at having involved my neighbour in that inchoate fantasy and having to admit that I was enjoying it. Four in the morning is a metro stop on the nocturnal trajectory I've been making in recent months. I get off there every time, I know it well and it knows me well. The overflowing bins, the ammonia that comes up from a ground that never looks clean. You breathe in a gulp of dark station air and reveal all your fears. Sometimes I only stop there to play at who can keep their eyes closed the longest, other times to hear the brushing of eyelashes on the pillowcase, or the seconds that hide behind the glass of the alarm clock. I often miss the train. I miss it when, even though I've learnt the theory and know that I shouldn't peel my arms off the sides of my body, I extend one to the left and find the mattress empty.

I wash my face and get back into bed with my mouth dry and my head slightly aching. My heart skips a beat. The telephone in my dream is a real name on my mobile's screen: Pep. Missed call.

Six minutes past four in the morning. A strange time to call someone, but I can't miss more trains, so I take a deep breath and release it like someone preparing for something very important that requires much concentration. I line up my thoughts into one single one, sigh and press his name. Pick up, please. And he picks up.

"Paula?"

"Hi, Pep. Sorry to call so late. But you just called me, right?" My voice comes out hoarse, and more timid than I'd like. I clear my throat and close my eyes, like devout women close them when penitently saying the Lord's Prayer and two Hail Marys. We try to spark up a conversation, involving pragmatic things that interest neither of us, about missed calls and how late it is. Who cares about time zone differences when the impact of a long-awaited call is hitting you like a meteorite crashing into Earth?

"Is everything OK, Paula?"

"Of course," I lie quickly. "I just called to see about getting together." I can't make my voice sound less scared and, now that I'm airing what's been locked up inside me for so many days, I feel ridiculous all the way down to my bone marrow, to the point of feeling I should apologize. "Forgive me, I was asleep," I add with a small sound that attempts to be a laugh.

"But is everything OK?"

"Yeah, sure…"

"…"

"Listen, Pep, I think I owe you an apology."

There is an uncomfortable silence broken only by a nasal sound on the other end of the line. I can't tell him the truth. I can't underestimate the power and the potency of a word as thick as *death*.

"Paula, it's been a long time." There is no trace of reproach in his tone but he doesn't finish the sentence, leaving me room to explain.

"I know. I'm sorry. I don't know what to say."

"I was worried that something had happened to you."

I cover my face with one hand.

"I'd like to see you. Do you think that's possible?"

He sighs.

"You won't suddenly disappear?" Now the silence belongs to me. I hadn't got that far, I hadn't got past the need for a body to sustain me and it makes me realize how frivolous and selfish I've been since Mauro's been gone. "That was a joke, Paula," he adds with his usual confidence. "Are you sure you're OK?"

"I have some evenings free before my next shift. When would be good for you?"

"Right now I'm in Boston. I'll probably be back for New Year's, I don't have a ticket yet. I'll call you when I get back. OK?"

Boston. Life has continued while I was stopped, stuck. I wanted to ask him what the hell he was doing in Boston, if there's some eco-house in the works, or if he has someone waiting for him in a small flat with snow at the door who, when he arrives in the evening, covered in oak shavings, shouts, "Darling, there's cold chicken in the fridge!" but I don't dare overstep the boundaries.

"OK."

"Talk to you soon, then."

"Pep!" I add, about to lose my cool.

"Yes?"

"Thank you."

He draws out the wait, pausing a little too long before responding.

"Thank you for calling."

Boston. I stretch out on the bed and fix my gaze and the conversation on the ceiling to study it in detail. It was lame and short but I just talked to Pep on the phone and the oneiric metro station is surprised to find me relaxed and laughing. It's an old dormant feeling that awakens now to let me know that I've moved forward one step, that I've found a clue on the path out of the cave, that my self-destruction is postponed. At least until New Year's. Suddenly the shadow pulls on my pyjama sleeve and spits in my face. Where do you think you're going, so happy? Leave me be, I order it, and that night, surprisingly, it keeps quiet.

* * * * * *

You were focused on reading an original manuscript in bed. The laptop lit up between us, your glasses on the tip of your nose, your immaculate pyjamas, my feet tangled up with yours. Outside on the terrace, the automatic sprinkler programmed for eleven thirty, the waxing crescent moon, the alarm clocks set so I would leap out of bed at seven twenty, and you five minutes later. Our careers were consuming, and the little time we spent together was in that pleasurable but prosaic space created by two adults with no children. We'd grown used to silence, to a tidy house, to the Vietnamese restaurant in the Eixample, the Japanese one in Gràcia, to order, and the selfish pleasure of that being enough. And periodically, like a monsoon season that's feared but expected, we would fight over your desire to be a father, completely incompatible with my vague, laconic maternal instinct. Like good mammals, our relationship was governed by our ability to communicate with each other, providing us with benefits like food, rest, safety and company. It wasn't our thing, Mauro, all couples require that. We had learnt to communicate through chemical, physical, visual and tactile means, but as the years went by, we no longer looked each other in the eye when explaining things, we didn't touch each other constantly when passing the oil cruet at meals, or taking

110

the other's arm for balance while we tied our shoes. I was comfortable with that bare minimum of love necessary to impel our relationship forward, and I didn't know any other way of loving. But we loved each other. I also loved you the night that I tore the manuscript out of your hands.

"Check this out, Mauro, it's so good!"

You groaned. I'd made you lose your place but I shushed you, captivated.

The astronaut Chris Hadfield, commander on board the International Space Station, had posted a video that was going viral, that showed how your tears don't fall in space. The lack of gravity makes the liquid progressively accumulate in your eyes and remain at the bridge of your nose.

Together we watched as the astronaut made the tears move from one eye to the other. Then we saw another where the same astronaut sings David Bowie's "Space Oddity". He drifts inside the International Space Station spinning the guitar, in zero gravity, while outside you can see the Earth covered by the atmosphere and dots of human light that fill the spread of continents with warmth. You moved your fingers on the laptop to the beat of the music, you liked Bowie, you liked him a lot.

"It's incredible," you said.

"I knew you'd like it," I replied, pleased at having being able to entertain you.

"It's incredible how, while down here it's all about going to work and following the same herd of sheep, day after day, looking forward to a holiday in some tourist destination jammed with people for a few miserable weeks in the summer, up there a few lucky guys are floating through space and have a completely different perspective. Outer space exists, at least for them."

If I had been paying more attention, I would have got offended at that point, Mauro, I should have said that, as the black sheep in your herd, I hoped I brought a little fun and affection into your life. I could have said that we weren't so badly off; I believed that at the time, didn't you? I could have promised you I would change some of my work shifts, that I knew other verb tenses beyond the conditional. But all I did was smile at the guitar floating and spinning at the International Space Station, and make some ridiculous comment about Commander Hadfield's moustache.

"If I could be born again, I wouldn't work in publishing. I'd be an astronaut." You took off your glasses and looked at me, nodding your head, very convinced. "Really, Paula, I mean it. I'd be an astronaut."

Born again. You had to die to be born again as a memory. *Astronaut* comes from the Greek words *astro*, which means star, and *nautes*, which means sailor. Are you anything now? Where are you? You must be an astronaut. You're a good man, Mauro. Someone should grant you that last wish. "Come back," I ask you sometimes, "please come back, even to be with her." But nothing makes sense, Mauro. Only this feeling of incompleteness.

* * * * * *

9

"Good morning, Santi! I brought you a butter croissant, the kind you like… And, best of all, home-brewed coffee."

For years, Santi and I have shared a caffeine addiction. During my first night as a neonatologist, we overlapped in the break room. His tired face contrasted with mine, filled with the excitement of my first shift. He was standing in front of the coffee machine, tall as a giraffe, and I waited impatiently behind him as the roasted, volatile aroma invaded the small space. I had a thousand questions for him, but I had to hold them in. I'd already been asking him questions all night. I was desperate for the chance to leap out of my chair to attend to some cardiac arrest, anxious for a resuscitation in the delivery room or something, anything, I just had to finally act on my desire to be needed. He was the one who sparked our bonding over coffee.

"Do you know that caffeine not only keeps you awake but stimulates your memory?"

"Yes, it stimulates certain memories, and generates a resistance to forgetting. And there's more: it also improves your response time. You need less cerebral activation to carry out a task requiring attention. In fact, with a dose as small as seventy-five milligrams, you can already see significant improvements," I said in a rapid burst.

He turned towards me, stunned, lifted a white eyebrow, and looked at me as if I were from another planet. I shrugged. I also wanted to explain that I thought it was brilliant how someone had dubbed the medication used to prevent apnea in babies *caffeine*, but it was our first casual conversation and I figured there was no need to highlight my eccentric vein.

The machine finished its process and he grabbed the hot cup by the upper edge with two fingers, careful not to burn himself, and lifted it in a celebratory toast.

"To your first shift. May all of them be this calm! And to coffee, or whatever the nasty liquid from this machine is."

I just smiled. I didn't dare say I wasn't hoping for calm, I didn't know how to articulate how anxious I was for responsibility, to put into practice all I'd learnt as a resident, to get a whiff of risk, I didn't know how to tell him that I was seduced by the idea of working at a tremendous pace and would have preferred a toast to hectic and exhausting shifts. Over the years we've met up many times in front of the coffee machine, and when the night is a rough one we're both comforted by the memory of that first night. So sometimes, when I come in at eight and I know Santi will be getting off his shift, I like to bring him some nice coffee and take care of him a little.

I didn't sleep many hours but, considering my sleep quality stats these last few months, I'm well above average. I woke up feeling alive, wanting to believe that things will be different. With Pep's call on the horizon, I felt change looming this morning.

I came into the hospital in a better mood, changed quickly, and pulled the coffee and croissant out of the bag. When I turned around I noticed that Santi was with some young guy who had no lab coat on, only a hospital badge. They were just standing beside the round meeting table, staring at me.

"Good morning, Dr Cid. Come here, I want to introduce you to Eric."

He calls me Dr Cid when things get hairy for one reason or another, otherwise I'm just Paula.

The Eric in question extended his hand and held mine as Santi reminded me that he's an osteopath who, through a university agreement, proposed a study on the role of touch in osteopathic manual therapy in premature infants.

"Eric will be here periodically for a year and a half."

I forced a smile. Santi had already told me about this, but I was convinced the Ethics Committee wouldn't green light it. I don't like when the hospital allows in professionals who aren't on the staff, and I don't like that Santi has waited until now to tell me the study had already been approved, now when the osteopath's right here in front of me, his legs spread too widely and his thorax as prominent as an Olympic weightlifter's, equal parts young and nervous. His hand is sweating, how in the hell is he supposed to treat my babies?

I know I shouldn't judge people too quickly. I also know I can't throw down the croissant and go for his jugular, but for a few seconds I consider it seriously.

"Paula, Eric was just telling me that, in addition to the organic and somatic aspects, he would like to work on the emotional and relational areas as well. Isn't that right, Eric?"

"Well, yes… to the degree that it's possible I believe it will be very interesting and useful to prove to what extent tactile interventions have a central role not only in diagnosis and osteopathic treatment but also in the development of therapeutic relationships with the patient."

They both looked at me, waiting for a reaction. It didn't seem appropriate to say that I thought the logic of that was so overwhelming it was ridiculous to carry out a study to prove it. I just stood there with my arms folded across my chest.

"As I mentioned to you before, Paula, we will focus the study on two of the four infants who are in the NICU continuously. Having taken a detailed look at their clinical histories, Eric feels that the most interesting cases would be Ivet and Mahavir. We've explained the project to the parents and they're on board."

"Eric, would you excuse us for a moment?"

I gently pulled Santi by the elbow, over to the computer area. With my back to Eric, I interrogated Santi with my gaze and, almost without moving his jaw, he conveyed please, do me this favour, we discussed this, and any and all research at the hospital is a good thing.

"Mahavir…" I left my complaint hanging in the air. If I said that I'm the only one who can touch him, my childishness would send Santi into a rage.

I felt him firmly pushing me back over to the young man, who despite appearances was managing to tolerate stoically that uncomfortable parenthesis.

"Dr Cid," Santi added sternly, "after the change-of-shift report, find a lab coat for Eric. He'll be starting today."

Vanesa and Marta had appeared in the room, speaking amongst themselves in their usual chipper tone, but they were suddenly silent when they saw the osteopath. Marta was undressing him with her eyes and I couldn't help rolling mine. They introduced themselves, as if Santi and I weren't there. Their over-the-top flirtatiousness, which the young man seemed to eat up, made me feel invisible, right there in my own ward. As if that weren't enough, it turned out that it was a small world and the osteopath and Vanesa had summered together over several years, so that dominated the conversation, which was the final straw for me. Santi and I had been left in the background, and I gave him the paper bag with the croissant and the thermos of coffee without saying a word.

"Come on, Paula. Don't be like that."

"Like what? I don't like having people I don't know milling around the NICU and playing with the babies. Have you considered the added stress for them of being moved once more each day?"

"The psychology team has approved it, and the parents want to take part in the study. You have to be more flexible, Paula."

"The psychology team? And what about the rehab people, what did they say?"

117

"I don't think this is the right time to discuss this. You are a great doctor, Paula, but you don't respect the line."

"What line are you talking about, Santi?"

Just then, a little further away, the osteopath said something that made Marta burst out laughing.

"I've been telling you for some time now that you need to slow down and work less, take some time to reflect on what happened. Working more shifts than the two residents combined isn't helping you, Paula."

"Santi!" I said, peeved. "Your paternalistic tone is starting to wear on me. I told you I'm fine. And besides, why are you bringing this up again now?"

He thought it over briefly. The first rays of December sun were coming directly through the wide slats of the blinds and right into his eyes. He put up one hand as a visor and took his time to reply.

"The hospital is not your home, Paula, and these babies are not your children."

I swallowed hard and lowered my head. I noticed Santi's shoes. My father has an identical pair. Comfortable, old man shoes, with a good rubber sole to absorb impact and adapt to feet in motion. Entirely unconcerned with aesthetics, they are the shoes of someone who knows his place in the world and values pragmatism over anything else. He took a few steps with those wise feet, over to the others, and left me surrounded by the echo of his statement.

"Come on, ladies, I want to go home," he said. "Let me update you for the shift."

The osteopath waited in a corner, not knowing what to do while Santi spoke to us. I pretended not to be affected by this attack of sincerity from the man who had watched me grow as a professional, I even smiled when he offered to the junior doctors the coffee I had brought him from home and joked that he hoped their time with us had at least taught them how to take care of their future staff as well as Paula did. Some people excel at their job but suck at apologies.

Not your home and not your children. I didn't want to consider his words, I didn't even let them past my upper temporal lobe and into the Wernicke's area, where auditory information is transformed into units of meaning. I can't accept them as a unit of meaning. I refuse to. What does he know?

Once Santi had left, Marta went on a mile a minute, teasing me about the osteopath. Don't be stupid, don't hold back, you should hit on him, he's hot AF. What is everyone's problem?

"Enough! Cut it out, Marta. Where do you think you work? Remember we still have to do a diagnostic on the girl in three. You can't go home until you've got it figured out. Vanesa, get going on Raquel's tests. I need them before two. And get a move on, the clock's ticking!"

They looked at me, shocked. Marta gave me a nasty look while Vanesa hurried off with her head bowed. The osteopath was sitting in a chair, his eyes wide.

"You!"

"Yes, Paula." He leapt up.

"No, not Paula. Dr Cid. Is that clear? Follow me."

With utmost perversity, I pushed into his face a lab coat that was a whole size too small, conscious that I would never have done that before. Maybe that was my new identity: lonely, irritable woman whose only joy in life is work, who has Sunday lunch every week with her father, a former advertising jingle composer who doesn't let her leave until they decide whether to lower the saccharine new melody he's named "Bella" by a half-tone or add in a C sharp. Lonely woman who jogs a little further each day trying to combat her insomnia, who spends her time reading scientific magazines and staring at her mobile hoping to see the name of a carpenter who hasn't called; lonely woman who doesn't want to have a forty-third birthday party because she doesn't think there's anything more to celebrate, who kisses the cold glass of a frame that holds a photo of happier times and Midsummer celebrations, and who occasionally spends Saturday evenings babysitting so her best friend Lídia can recoup some couple time now that the girls are bigger, so she can rediscover a silent, taciturn man who works in finance or something like that, but who is there, who exists, who smells of the cologne he was gifted last Christmas and fills a small percentage of the wardrobe with his straitlaced clothes. A husband who when he was young—not so long ago—smoked joints and did a great Julio Iglesias imitation, and who gradually, since he put on that tuxedo and promised Lídia he'd be faithful for richer and for poorer, in sickness and in health, to love and honour her for the rest of his life, had started smoking less, and once he held the first ultrasound image in his hands, gave up smoking and singing, and by the second he was well versed in birthing and baby food, and his conversations suffered. But he's there, after all these years, and no matter how much he's soured and put on the pounds, his presence means Lídia's not transparent, and when he arrives home she can tell him if there was traffic on the roads or if he needs to call someone to have a look at the noise from the stupid extractor fan. No matter how much the years have eroded him, he still wishes her a good night and wakes up every day by her side.

So this lonely despot could release the monster she's nurturing inside, a monster with no consideration, no values, no exciting future ahead, because what difference does all that make now? If it's just about getting out of bed and remembering to breathe, scruples probably only get in the way, and it'd be better to not expect anything from anybody.

I slammed the door hard and walked briskly beside the osteopath, smoke coming out of my ears, and stopped right before entering the NICU, panting.

"I'll be whoever I want to be, not let other people decide for me!" I shouted at him.

"What?" he asked, stunned.

I was so deep inside myself that I had lost sight of the world. I can't prove Santi right. I have to stop living in my fantasies and start paying attention to what's going on around me. I could take some pills, something for my nerves at least, or for sleeping, drug myself, but there's no need to medicalize every situation, my situation is just life, just life that goes on and gets stuck. You've explained it millions of times to parents of patients who don't make it or who've been living in hospital for months on end. Remember what you tell them, Paula, that they should go to the beach, have some seafood in the Barceloneta with the winter sun on their faces, that the babies will be in good hands. I closed my eyes and forced myself to imagine the sea.

"Dr Cid? Are you feeling OK?"

The osteopath touched my shoulder. When I opened my eyes, there he was, with a concerned expression and in that white coat he could hardly button up. Given the size of his thorax, it looked like he was wearing the costume of a superhero about to evolve into a higher state of supernatural strength and energy. I was overcome by a fit of laughter. He must have thought I was off my rocker, and the truth is, after my outburst, there wasn't much I could say to defend myself against the charge.

"Please forgive my behaviour."

"It's fine, really, it's fine, Dr Cid," he repeated, totally bewildered.

"Paula. You can call me Paula. I thought my day was off to a good start, but, hey... I'm sorry."

"I completely understand, don't worry."

I swallow my desire to tell him he doesn't understand a thing.

"Welcome to the NICU, Eric. Hands nice and clean, loosen your lab coat a little, and you'll be ready to meet my tiny treasures. Before we go in I want to make one thing clear." He nodded, expectantly. "I'm not convinced about your study."

"But the doctor told me that the team had agreed and I thought that…"

"No, I never agreed. I don't have anything against your discipline, quite the opposite, but I'm not convinced that it's what these babies need right now."

He bowed his head slightly, submissive, and then looked frankly into my eyes.

"Thank you for your sincerity. I understand the disruption and objections that can arise from having someone who isn't part of your team working directly with the children, but I am one hundred per cent convinced about what I do. Trust me."

Trust. Trust, Paula, trust him, trust that "the species that survive are not the strongest or most intelligent, but those who best adapt to change." Change, Paula.

I held out my hand and he shook it. I opened the door and invited him in. Santi can say whatever he wants, but when I step onto this unit's sound-muffling floor, I'm home.

* * * * * *

The black widow lives alone twelve months a year, with one macabre exception: she sometimes kills and eats her partner after copulation, in a violent mating ritual that led to her name.

There's also Hanna Glawari, *The Merry Widow*, imagined by Viktor Léon and Leo Stein for Franz Lehár's operetta in three acts. Hanna is young and lovely and left millions by her husband, and has to remarry for matters of state.

And then there's me. Since we were never actually married, and I'm not an arachnid, I'm left without a proper label to help me fit into this world of the living, where it seems everything has to be classified and archived.

But there must be some place for me in this wide world. There are no spiders in Antarctica, no spiders in the air, no spiders in the sea.

* * * * * *

We were searching for a flat to rent, based on neighbour-hood and price. We prioritized location, wanting silence at night and everything close by during the day. Mauro was after a terrace, I wanted light. We each chased our dreams, separately, in our careers. Buying a flat together seemed too much like an engagement ring, like a marriage certificate, or a dog you know you'll outlive because the canine lifespan is about twelve years. My father was more in favour of buying, like so many people who come from a humble background and do well for themselves, he'd been anxious to own. My circumstances are similar, but I've never wanted to buy a flat. I've always remembered how every promise of permanence can be snatched away with no warning, how everything that fills can suddenly empty out with the violence of a curettage. It happens with mothers, with flats, with dogs, it happens with love.

I would often gaze up at the facades of larger flats in other parts of Barcelona, eyes glazed as if looking into a mirage. Leaving the neighbourhood was a desire within reach. I was fully aware that it would mean distancing myself from Sant Antoni's amalgam of familiar flavours and immigrant col-ours, where I'd lived since I was a little girl. I'd always been captivated by the varied life swirling around the market, the languages that fragmented and came together again as they evolved into a new tongue, a vibrant, shifting reality, but now, as an adult, I was irritated by all the noisy construction, and by the exorbitant prices for flats and groceries. I was sick of the streets lined with cookie-cutter bars that had mercilessly forced out the quaint businesses that had been there forever, and above all I was uncomfortable with my past. I was convinced that life was happening elsewhere. I went to the other extreme, an immaculate island in Barcelona's uptown where most of the inhabitants lived facing the glazed galleries that overlooked their inner courtyards. Unsettling silences grew behind the doors, behind the masks of retouched lips and polished loafers. Conservative characters, many of them forged by and clinging to an unreal economic security, who live far from any possibility of subversion, frozen, dozing in their own dreams. On Sundays it's surprising to see how many people gather around the churches, well-coiffed very young folk, cut from the same cloth, entire families with many children crammed with orthodontics, and wearing matching polo shirts and oversized satin bows atop their heads. I wonder what they ask Christ for, or what they confess to him, or what they thank him for. Afterwards they buy roast chicken and bring it back to their homes. During the ski season and summer, the neighbourhood is emptied of families and all you see are elegant elderly women with dogs that are cleaner and better fed than the child population of the Horn of Africa.

I went there to reinvent myself. I felt defined by Sant Antoni and what I wanted was to fade into the background, though I didn't fully realize that until I left. I'd accepted a staff position at the hospital and it seemed the right moment to modulate the image I projected, too. My father had raised me to better myself, and with the change of neighbourhood I was convinced I was leaving behind studious Paula who knew the scientific name for every bird, and that, with my new salary, I could adopt a bourgeois patina. And I was also convinced that, along the way, I could make him happy. People make progress, in large part, to satisfy their parents' wishes. Moving to a neighbourhood above the Avinguda Diagonal was like acquiring a new status. A fake one, but a new one nonetheless. I wasn't interested in the people there, I didn't want to be like them, I figured I'd just be different. Betray my roots to project a slightly better image. Allow myself the luxury of strolling down clean streets focused on my fleeting fripperies. It lent me a borrowed happiness, and that was enough for me. But long before I could afford to change neighbourhoods and had to share the rent with a translator from Càceres who played the flute night and day, my eyes were already making their way up past balcony railings and I would imagine myself inside, all alone, getting to and from the hospital on a beat-up motorcycle I'd park on the corner. But then one day you really fall in love for the first time in your life. You're thirty years old. You secrete dopamine, serotonin and oxytocin, and you start to soften. You leave behind the flautist from Càceres and, in order not to ask your dad for money, you're willing to share another flat, one you'd stared wistfully at many times, with its horizontal and vertical symmetry, its rose-tinted sgraffito and ornamental border decorating part of the facade. Mauro is enigmatic and intelligent, and he fascinates you. You give in when you put his underwear into the washer along with your favourite cotton shirt, when you drive a car instead of a motorcycle, when you go together to the places that used to be your private getaway spots, when you meet his family and introduce him to your truncated and anomalous one, but you also have to give up overthinking things.

I didn't give in about the mortgage, we rented our flat and it welcomed us in and adapted to our subdued way of loving each other. Thinking that Mauro was mine made me reflect long and hard. Getting married would be the same as buying a flat, and not getting married was more like renting. So I rented a man, an attentive man with glasses and a certain old-fashioned air. I didn't know if I liked having him in the sense of possessing him, I liked him now, in the present, and that was all. I liked our conversations, the things he read to me, how his temper flared over politics, and how he got involved with things: he saved plants and animals and donated money to ecological organizations. From our bedroom, I often watched him working on the terrace on his days off. One summer morning, when we'd only been living together for a few years, he came in from outside with his forehead pearled with sweat. He had damp dirt under his nails and a small rake in his hand. He talked about coming back from holiday, the autumn, celebrating something with friends, "I planted strawberries," he said, "right here." He shot me a fearful glance that spoke of commitment. You give in while love secretes chemicals and then the autumn comes too fast, the leaves fall from the trees and a ring falls onto your finger. After we'd lived together for some time, my brain still had a few drops of phenethylamine, a chemical compound in the amphetamine family that led me to accept the jewel gracefully and stifle the tsunami of concern raging inside. At the hospital I took off the ring as soon as I arrived and left it in my locker with my handbag and clothes. The newborns' fragility was the excuse that turned that treacherous gesture into an innocent one. The ring: a circle, without beginning or end. A threat of eternal matrimony. Engaged Paula locked up for a few hours. Years later I scarcely noticed it and the small groove it had left on my ring finger, even though I'd already twice said no, I didn't want to get married. He stopped asking. We got angry. We made up. We carried on. The decorative border on the door, the terrace, the light, the ring on my finger, his underwear and mine spinning endlessly and then, gradually, desire filtered down the drain and everything became a comfortable, involuntary, completely mechanical calm. The ring stored away. It was enough to say something about the size, it doesn't fit, I'll wear it on occasions, the ones deemed special, while I knew I was trapped in so-called normality, a stable relationship, a shared life, Stockholm Syndrome. We'd both given in to the other so many times that we didn't even realize how we were holding each other back. It wasn't anyone's fault. It just happens.

—

I'm at Thomas's flat. He's sleeping. I glance down at the streets of our neighbourhood, lethargic at this time of the morning. There are already Christmas lights up. Christmas. My heart comes up in my throat like a gulp of sour milk, but I swallow it back down. That morning I decided to put on my engagement ring, knowing I would see Lídia. I haven't worn it for many years and it feels as heavy on my finger as ever. I move my thumb inside my palm to turn the jewel that has been stored away for so long. It adapts to me seamlessly, as if no one ever shattered the circle.

Lídia was at my place a few hours ago. I went Christmas shopping with her. She's become someone who thinks ahead. I liked her much better before, when she protested in the halls of our university and improvised medical expeditions to remote places with no electricity or running water. I don't tell her that.

"Have you thought about your birthday celebration?"

"Come on, Lídia, don't start. You and Toni and the girls can come over for dinner, and that'll be that."

"No way. We'll throw a proper party. Without the girls, please. I don't want the girls anywhere near. And we'll see about Toni."

"You can be such a pain."

She came up to the flat grumbling about the cold. In front of the mirror she put on and took off a jacket three times. She wasn't convinced about the colour. She spent a couple of hours bringing me up to speed on a world that, in a way, no longer interested me. She talked about birthdays, films, restaurants, filled me in on private arguments with some of the other mothers at school, how sick she is of dealing with them.

"Don't you remember, I told you how that stupid class representative goes around acting like she's the Senate majority leader?"

I stop listening to her and ponder whether I would be able to keep track of who were the class representatives at my hypothetical daughters' school. My hypothetical daughters would have to constantly remind me. My hypothetical daughters would have to remind me each morning that I'm a mother at all. Lídia insists she can't stand the woman, that when she runs into her on the street and says hi the idiot ignores her, but that she couldn't care less, she's not really involved with the class mothers, she's got enough on her plate, although some of the mums are now trying to convince her to go up to Montserrat to work on a nativity scene on the last day before Christmas break.

"Can you imagine me climbing a mountain to put the baby Jesus in a cradle?"

She leapt from one subject to the next as she opened up the shopping bags. Lately she's done nothing but complain, about work, that it's nonstop, check-ups all day long and seeing kids with common colds brought in by hysterical mothers convinced snot is a sign of terminal illness. She complains about her parents, who've started to forget if it's Tuesday or Friday when they have to pick up the girls at school; she complains about her husband, who according to her has become some kind of a magic trick, now you see him now you don't; she complains about the construction work on her street; that her coffee is cold, that her woollen sweater itches. She complains. Lídia is increasingly irritable and I struggle to find traces of the confidence she used to exude. She's angry with life, which has been very good to her. Some people shine when there are problems to be solved, but when things go well they wither, get bored, and the aura that made them special fades away. There's no point in denying that friendships also age, like books, like films, they can suddenly seem so passé. The thought makes me miserable. I can't lose more people I love, so I force myself to listen to her.

She sat me down on the edge of my bed. She tried out some eyeshadow on me, saying it would accentuate my enig-matic gaze. I looked at her sceptically, but she continued, determined. I also let her put mascara on my lashes and a limited-edition blusher called Orgasm. She winked at me. I let her do my make-up, my eyes closed and her monologue a relentless soundtrack as she held my face gently. The touch of her fingers on my skin made her voice fade into the back-ground. When I was twelve I got braces, and on the days when my father had deadlines that meant hours and hours locked in his study, he would send me to the orthodontist alone. He composed jingles for television and radio when original advertising music was having a good moment. I had got used to living with just my dad but, even still, him not coming with me to the orthodontist was a tragedy. I never told him, but I felt panicked. Not only was it painful when they adjusted my braces by twisting wires behind my molars, but I was also the only girl in the waiting room alone, trembling and embarrassed about the nurse calling out my name. All those placid mothers observed me, and the occasional father, but mostly mothers, turning magazine pages, impassive within the circle of their normality, and giving mechanical replies to their respective progeny. They smelt good, wore pearls and bracelets that jangled when they fixed a poorly folded collar or tied shoelaces. They were sweet mothers, mother shields, tiger mothers. They were mothers in a waiting room. But the appointments themselves gave me a feeling of tenderness I haven't felt since, perhaps because my need for affection waned as I grew up, but the fact is that that gentleness, of the hygienist's hands on my face as she placed the cold tools in my mouth in preparation for the orthodontist, remains unparalleled. I felt moved by the delicacy of her fingers, rescuing me from the small tragedy of every visit. My father did a pretty good job, in his role as widower, but he's never been a physically demonstrative man. I didn't know that I needed that affection until I found myself immersed in the antiseptic scent of the dentist's chair. Lídia's fingers feel the same way on my face, as she does my make-up.

"Paula… have you gone to sleep?… Listen, where should I leave this stuff? It looks better on you than on me."

She put the blusher away in a dresser drawer, still talking a blue streak, and then, suddenly, she grew silent. We were trapped in a silence like the calm before a storm, when birds fly lower and all the animals that sense it run off, terrified.

"Paula, the ring!"

She pulled it out of its green velvet box, and when she closed it the sound of the tiny hinges was like thunder. Inevitable storm.

A ring.

A terrace filled with friends.

Laughter.

Shared confidences.

We ate.

We drank.

We were still secreting.

The plants grew lush.

We decorated.

We celebrated.

We lived.

"I stopped wearing it years ago. It was really small on me," I said, feigning indifference but looking at the jewel out of the corner of my eye.

"You think I didn't notice? I always thought it was gorgeous."

A small, round diamond solitaire, sober and elegant. She's right, it's gorgeous.

"Put it on, Paula."

"What are you saying?" I protested.

We stare at each other. First I count ten freckles on her nose to keep from getting worked up, but she seeks out my gaze and those blue eyes of hers become a mirror. I see myself all alone, with no kids, no dog, not even any plants, holding up a ring that's nothing when closed up in a box. Yet, when I try to go further, when I continue deciphering the nuances in her blue gaze, I realize the ring on my finger would position me, give me a place, save me uncomfortable explanations. For practical purposes, the ring would blurt out a name for me: widow.

"Mauro loved you very much, Paula. Anyone can have an existential crisis, especially at this age. You were the love of his life."

"That's enough, Lídia, please, stop."

But she doesn't. She pulls a tiny ball off her woollen pullover and rolls it between two fingers while talking about "that girl" who she claims wouldn't have lasted long, and I regret having told her about the ballerina's existence, and inside I count how long "not long" is, whether all the months they were together could be considered "not long", if all the plans for the future saved up in Mauro's mobile fit within that "not long".

"I talked to Pep, over the phone." I spit it out like phlegm to halt her attempt to organize a life for me that no longer exists. The sea of her eyes seems to calm. She smiles and lifts one brow, curious. "Maybe we'll see each other at the end of the year."

Patches of blue between clouds appear in her gaze and despite everything I start to have palpitations again. I've been having them for days. My body has become an armoured shell, capable of attacking the trenches to keep advancing, but with the end of each war I discover small internal wounds weakening me, confirming my resistance is waning. I wonder how long this war will last and how long I will be standing.

It's pitch black. I must break free, make the stifling hours advance, invoke the spring, the daylight, go to work. I brought the laptop to the sofa, in pyjamas, I still have the make-up on, intact like a clown in the dressing room after a performance. A clown with a ring on her finger. I drink wine, a second glass. I try to remember if I used to drink so assiduously. I know I didn't, but I pretend to be wracked with doubt. When you're alone, it's important to maintain a certain amount of dialogue with yourself, put yourself between a rock and a hard place, not just let yourself get away with everything. Five minutes and the alcohol is already in my blood. The plan is to lie here and let the ethanol depress my central nervous system, make me drowsy, lower the intensity of my cerebral and sensory functions, but the plan fails, a little bit like everything, in the end, and I decide to give in to my curiosity and type the word *widow* into Google Images. Basically, I come up against two stereotypes: sad, lonely older ladies, some but not all of them dressed in black, and attractive young women, man-eaters who make it clear they're back on the market. It seems there are two valid ways to embody this new label but neither one seems right for me. I vaguely remember another widow, a plant Mauro and my dad talked about one afternoon when we were hiking around the Sant Pere de Rodes monastery.

I looked for it too, and I found it. I can see them both talking, with their shorts and rucksacks, pointing at that purplish pink flower with long bristles opened in a star, as I sat on a low wall waiting impatiently for it to be time for a swim at the Clisques beach before sunset. That day there was no way I could know that I would carry the name of a spider or a flower embroidered invisibly on a stretch of my skin.

I finish the wine in one gulp. I scan the headlines, I can't get past them. The world no longer interests me. I reread a couple of work emails and open the photos my father sent me of the paella he made on Sunday with his friends. My present is a desert.

I grab the bottle of wine, another glass and the keys. I swing up to Thomas's flat.

"Look at me. Do I look like a widow?"

"It's fucking late, Paula! Come on in..." he says in English.

His flat smells of tobacco. I ask him if his extractor fan is working. He scratches his head and with drowsy slow words, half asleep, he asks me which I want him to answer first, the question about how I look or the one about the fan. He's got bedhead and I giggle. I like his impossible hair. I blow on his fringe. He mumbles something I don't catch while he puts on a Stevie Wonder record, delicately pinching the needle and letting it drop gently onto the disc. I hold out a glass of wine to him. The record player starts its reading and the friction regales us with the crackle of the needle gliding along the grooves. I ask him why we marginalized a sound of that magnitude in the evolution of our species. We both agree it is museum-worthy, and drink a toast to that. Preoccupied, he tells me what I already know about his lease ending soon and him having to give up the flat because the owner wants to give it to his daughter who's getting married, as a gift. We look at the space surrounding us, in silence. I brush his shoulder and promise him that I'll come visit him wherever he ends up. Once we're filled with wine we start to dance to "Part-Time Lover", still sitting on the sofa. We move our torsos and shoulders, our arms and hands, but we're exhausted and incapable of getting up. He blows smoke rings and I break them with my fingers to the rhythm of the music. His eyes are red. I know he's staying awake just for me.

We are two adults, like so many others, who remain outside familiar circuits, motherhood, fatherhood, spouses. Two adults who live without any intimate commitment to any other human being. We are free, or perhaps we are prisoners of our freedom. I know that the blonde woman with the leather trousers sleeps here some nights, only some. It's Thomas who chooses when he wants company and when he wants to continue as a lonely soul within the big city. Is that what I'll do from now on? Is that what I would have done if Mauro were still alive? Thomas chooses to be alone. When I didn't want to renounce my solitude, I suddenly came across a person who filled it all up, dissolving the individuality I used to wake up with each morning, and I learnt to adapt to my own contradiction. You share a kiss, a private corner, a confidence, a flat, and you end up sharing an entire life. Up to a certain point everything is in our hands, one way or another we control the inertia, until fate does what it does, leaving behind a random bunch of distorted memories and the impotence of not being able to go back or continue forward. My solitude can't be like Thomas's because I'm expected to change, plaster and paint over the gash life decided to furrow into my back.

I want to hide here, with the weight of the wine on my eyelids, here where everything is veiled by the whitish grey of tobacco smoke and a solitary friend makes me listen to record after record of Eighties music.

I want to stay with the Thomas who musses my hair and tells me he's sleepy, that he has to get up early tomorrow and that, if I want, I can sleep on his sofa.

I ask him one more time, with pleading eyes, and he retells the story I like so much about how he left everything in New York and landed in Barcelona with empty pockets, inspired by a Juan Marsé novel. Mauro loved that story too. I like being the one who listens to it now, and it occurs to me again that perhaps that's what they mean when they say you can sense the dead, that other beings can remain alive inside you. Thomas talks of chosen families, of kilometres of distance, of reinventing yourself or dying. He stops telling the story for a moment to check if my eyes are closing and he whispers in English, "You don't look like a widow, you just look like a beautiful zombie."

And I sleep here, smiling, on a cinnamon-coloured sofa, beneath a blanket of questionable cleanliness. I sleep deeply, a couple of hours perhaps, until I'm awoken by the sound of rain on the street. I look at the buildings outside, only a couple of windows are faintly illuminated. This must be being alone. I'm afraid to be content with my solitude, because it reveals the desires I felt before meeting Mauro, it reveals that I can get through this. Being on your own provokes a different emotion, an invitation to life and resistance. The world belongs to the brave, I say to the coward reflected in the glass. I go back to my flat, willing to acknowledge that this solitude suits me. I pull the ring off my finger and put it back in the box. Forever more, this time.

Eric checks Mahavir's skull and abdomen, which is half the size of an adult palm. He manoeuvres the baby with his hands, very slowly, and touches him with extreme delicacy. I don't take my eyes off him. We've done four sessions and I still haven't confessed that I've noticed an improvement in Mahavir's abdominal distension and that on the days he works with him, the baby is intensely relaxed. But the osteopath with the prominent thorax wants to go further than just colic and explains that he still needs to explore the potential mechanisms of skin stimulation to provide both physiological and psychological benefits. I realize that I'm having trouble holding his gaze and I need to keep putting my hair behind my ears or bringing my hand to the nape of my neck, as if not paying much attention. When he says "positive impact" I scratch a section of skin behind my ear, which doesn't actually itch in the slightest. I lose control somewhat when I see him focused, his hands inside the incubator and touching Mahavir as if he could disintegrate at any moment and slip through his fingers. His intensity while working disturbs me, I feel a kind of envy. He is wearing the old, worn-out string and leather bracelets of a thirty-year-old fan of the Athletic Club of Bilbao with a paternal grandfather who still lives in Getxo, Basque Country. He was born in Barcelona but remembers the 1982–3 league on his grandpa's shoulders, cheering on the footballers from the shore. He tells me that while lowering his eyes in a way that makes him vulnerable, still clinging to the bond with his grandpa and with a football club. At Christmas he'll travel to Morocco with four friends. They haven't reserved hotels, they'll wing it, with rucksacks, he says. Let me come with you, I think desperately, but I just glance at the monitor. He isn't wearing a wedding ring. His skin is tanned even though it's winter and his hair curls slightly at the back of his neck as if he were still a boy. He's surrounded by the triumphant halo of a spoilt child who will do just fine in life, someone used to meeting goals, whose parents raised him with a rare mix of tenderness and discipline to believe he's the best. In a few short hours I'll learn that he rows in the Canal Olímpic, as the space separating our faces is foreshortened with words like portside and starboard. He will smell like mint gum trying to cover up the scent of tobacco, but that will be later on. Now he is silently handling Mahavir inside the incubator, until he turns and seeks out my eyes again.

"Do you think that today I could work the diaphragm area? He's very tense from constant crying and I think I could relax him. I know you've told me no many times and…"

"Go ahead," I say with a sudden burst of sympathy.

He looks at me with surprise and smiles gratefully and I clear my throat. I scratch again behind my ear where nothing itches, and finally I hide my nervous hands in the pockets of my scrubs and we don't say another word to each other.

142

The day has started to clear. There is a mist covering the flowerbeds in front of the hospital with a bluish light. When I'm about to get into my car I see the osteopath beside the car park exit. He's trying to light a cigarette as he cups his hands to protect it from the wind, his face tilted, his eyes squinted from the heat of the flame. I think about my neat, empty kitchen, about the insipid food, about the hum of the fridge. I remember the ballerina and I fantasize about the first steps she took to get close to Mauro. I close the car door and walk over to the osteopath without really knowing what I'm doing. I just want to feel as daring as she did.

"Hey, Eric. I saw you here… from over there." I turn to point to my car and can't believe how ridiculous I look and sound. He doesn't seem to mind. "Do you want a ride?"

"No, don't worry about me. I have my motorcycle. But thanks for the offer."

"Well, we can talk about it at the next session, but I just wanted to say that I've noticed an improvement in Mahavir, a very slight but definite improvement."

His face lights up. He exhales smoke, turning his face a little and twisting his lips to the left without taking his eyes off me, excited. I fill him in a little on the changes in the baby's vital signs.

"Wow! That makes me happy."

He tells me about a study done with chimpanzees separated from their mothers by a transparent screen that simulated an incubator.

"The chimpanzees could see, hear and smell their mothers, but they couldn't touch them." He pulls a strand of tobacco from the tip of his tongue with his little finger. "The study noted chronic activation in the HPA core, and it wasn't until they introduced physical contact with other infants," he pauses to exhale smoke again, "that the chimps who'd been separated by the screen began to develop normally."

I don't tell him that I'd read that study a few times, I let him think he's impressing me. I imagine the transparent screen and I hear the shrill cries of the agitated chimps futilely searching for contact with their mothers. Look at her, smell her, hear her, but don't touch her. She won't hold you. The cruelty of transparency. Suddenly it becomes unbearable to me. I take him by the arm and ask him if he's busy, I mean if he wants to celebrate Mahavir's improvements, with me.

He laughs almost soundlessly, with a frank innocence that's contagious, as if he had no plans, and wasn't surprised in the least by my reaction. He looks younger than ever and for the first time our roles are reversed, I'm waiting on an order from him, for him to make a decision. He stubs out what's left of the cigarette on an iron railing and takes a few steps away to throw it in a bin. In that distance between us, the outlines of where the night was heading begin to take shape.

"Where do you want to go?"

That's when he'll put some mint gum into his mouth and I'll draw closer to him, dying of embarrassment, to whisper into his ear I don't know but I'm cold. I follow a motorcycle to Sants and find parking with no problem. Go up crooked stairs, drink beer from a can in a flat I've never been in before. There is a fish tank lit up with a fluorescent bulb and an oar hung on the wall, a shelf with very few books and small objects carefully positioned: dice, glass marbles, trophies, a Rubik's cube and a graduation photo.

"Excuse the mess, I wasn't expecting guests."

He types something into his mobile and I imagine a hologram of Eric's four friends laughing at Eric's comment about having brought an older woman home. Define "older", they say, smirking inside. "I don't know, forty-something," and with four emojis they'll turn me into the anecdote of the year, and when they're atop some dune, when they've crossed the Atlas Mountains, they'll want to know if experience is a bonus and he'll tell them to piss off, scooping up a handful of fine cold sand in the desert morning and throwing it at them amid the shouts and laughter of men still teenagers at heart. Before the shadow can continue leading me down the path of self-destruction, I pull off my jeans, turtleneck jumper, spaghetti-strap camisole, socks and underwear. I get gooseflesh all over. The morning—when I put on the clothes now scattered over the floor—is so far away that it seems impossible it was still the same day as this one now.

"Tell me again about the therapeutic effects of touch."

He looks at me with attentive eyes and smiles timidly because he doesn't know I'm totally serious, and then everything becomes a knot of flesh and skin and tongues and we never leave that small living room and we do it on the sofa, where he must eat sushi made in a Chinese restaurant for supper and spend hours fiddling with his mobile. He moves too quickly and the sofa is too narrow, but it's good enough, I tell myself, it's good enough as a stimulus, Paula. That he wanted you even if just for this shag. I touch him to make sure he's there, because I don't hear anything. I grab him by the arse, I grip his shoulders, his breathing builds in intensity and now he's letting out short, muffled cries. Nothing, really. He is mint smoke and ash. He comes a few minutes later and drops his heavy head on my breasts and in that distance before in the car park, that space between where I stood and the bin, it had already been agreed that there would be no displays of affection, that the weight of his head against my body would reveal his innocence and my guilt, it had already been agreed that I would imagine Mauro alive and watching the whole scene and that I would look at him with revenge in my eyes, all alone and all empty. In that distance it had already been agreed that I would struggle to get home and to sleep, only to dream about chimpanzee babies pressing little hands against the transparent screen, shrieking with loneliness, hysterical from the absence of touch, desperate and punished with no hugs.

* * * * * *

You linger like something unresolved, that's how the energy feels; like those endless To Do lists you always made, lists of things we never found the moment for, remember?

- Organize the photo files.
- Set up autopay for the parking garage.
- Buy varnish to restore the table out on the terrace.
- Call the repairman about the noise from the extractor fan.

On the same list, I rack up rebukes I'll never voice to you, only to myself, and I suppose it must be normal, this pressure on my heart, filled with grievances and tears. When hating you doesn't work and I really want to weep, I use the muscles in my neck to hold back the tears, to keep myself from succumbing to a mood appropriate to my double tragedy. I go over each and every one of the neck muscles in a soft voice until I've managed to turn you into a cold anatomy poster, gradually distancing myself: sternothyroid, sternohyoid, sternocleidomastoid, I repeat in a relentless string, but you always come back, with your glasses on and the list of things to be done in one hand.

From bed I look out at the neglected terrace. All the plants have steadily died. How did you do it, Mauro? It must not have been enough just to water them. You talked to them. Not openly, never in front of other people. You said that talking to plants was a private, transformative act, an act of faith for those who don't believe in miracles. I get up, take a breath, and add to my list: Learn to talk to plants.

* * * * * *

This morning the sky has coral veins. I watched the sun come up, clutching a mug of coffee on the esplanade behind the hospital lobby at 8.17 a.m. I often come here in the morning when I work nights. It's a nice spot and there's no one else around at that time of the day except for the occasional staff member with a cigarette. Eric often comes out here to smoke but from now on we'll be careful not to meet outside the NICU. We didn't turn out to be a good match as lovers. There's no regret, and no desire to repeat. There's nothing, in fact. We avoid looking at each other and we focus on finishing the study, we concentrate on the power of his hands, which have provoked positive changes in the patients but trembled fearfully on my breasts and between my thighs. I'm an earthquake, frightening. It will be easy for us to forget it ever happened.

From up here you can see all of Barcelona, from east to west, and the first light of day tints the buildings silver. The sounds of the big city clump together in a single roar that sometimes seems to be calling me away from the hospital, but I don't want to leave yet. I have a missed call on my mobile. "Mauro Mother". The phone lets me know with a red 1 over the telephone icon. I haven't thought about anything else for a while now. The red catches your eye; in nature it represents a warning, of alarm or danger. Blood on a lioness's jaws after she's hunted fiercely for her cubs. If I leave the hospital I'll feel obliged to return her call immediately, if I stay for a while I can postpone the stomach ache and give myself time to imagine the possibilities. The first one that comes to mind is that someone else in his family has died, maybe his sister from ovarian cancer or a grandfather from a heart attack. The repetition of horror is a possibility I can't shake. I struggle to keep calm but, even still, decide to drag out my time here a little longer.

This morning we had a complicated birth. Severe hypoxia. We'll keep the baby on moderate therapeutic hypothermia and closely monitor her for a few days. I want to check on her once more before leaving. Good excuse, I tell myself. It's not my job to talk to her parents, but I can't get them out of my head. Yesterday, when I passed by the mother's room before she gave birth, she showed me some tiny flower-shaped earrings. Her eyes were filled with expectation and tenderness. A few hours later, all that's left in her gaze is stupefaction. I wonder how to reconcile two concepts as far from each other as a white gold flower with a tiny diamond in the centre and grave hypoxic-ischaemic encephalopathy. Life is like that, one day it shows you a pink-tinged sky and the next it's black night.

"Go home, Paula. You look tired." Teresa, the consultant responsible for the baby's follow-up care, examines my face professionally. Occupational hazard, we all take care of each other here like that. "I spoke to her parents, she's in a stable condition. You can relax."

"OK. I'll change and head out. Hope the day goes OK."

"And do me a favour, will you? Get some sleep. Oh, by the way!" she shouts, still walking. "You're coming to the dinner on Thursday, right?"

Dinner. Thursday. I note the date in my head and when Teresa turns down the hallway, carefree, her ponytail swinging, I sneak into the NICU.

The baby sleeps without earrings, her tiny intact earlobes like two lentils. She is adorned with other precious jewels, the adhesives stuck to her chest, the infusion pump and the electrode with a red light on her foot. The red 1 comes back into my head. I should call. They named her Alberta. The father explains that it was his great-grandmother's name. I didn't expect to find him here. Every time he looks at me I sense his red-rimmed eyes imploring me to promise that his daughter won't be damaged by all the possible consequences Teresa must have already explained. I avoid eye contact because I feel very tired, not up to offering the support needed by someone who's just had his future turned upside down. He is glued to the incubator, making me uncomfortable and unable to concentrate. I pretend to check the respirator so I can tell him that everything is working well. I head over to where Mahavir is.

"Hello, my little prince," I whisper, flush with the glass.

He's awake. He stretches out the fingers on both hands with small spasms and pulls one of his typical faces. I check the control sheets. My shift only ended an hour and a half ago and they've already put the CPAP back on him. I sigh loudly.

"Don't do this to me, kid. Didn't we promise we'd give it all we had?"

I cover up the incubator with the blanket that protects him from the light of the room and I slip away, disappointed, out the same door I came in through a moment earlier. I bump into Pili.

"What are you doing here?" she asks me in Spanish. "Didn't you work last night?"

"Hey, Pili… you scared me! I was just leaving. Listen, I'd like to do an echocardiogram on Mahavir this week. I want to rule out pulmonary hypertension again."

"The echocardiogram isn't urgent, is it? Besides, please don't order it if you haven't talked it over with the other doctors, you're making me batty with all these requests. Honestly, Paula. Go for a walk or have some breakfast by the sea, get some air, honey, but please get out of this hospital for a while."

She puts her plump hands into the pockets of her scrubs and gives me a look that's part compassionate and part scolding. It makes me blush. I didn't know it was so obvious. I don't know where to hang my hat. No one is waiting for me.

There are a lot of things I could ask Pili: whether she has five minutes, if she'll sit with me on the benches at the hospital entrance, whether her forecast for my short, medium and long term future beyond these hospital walls is complete and utter tedium. If she thinks I'm boring. If she thinks I should be covering up these grey hairs that have started sprouting mercilessly. If she knows what Mauro's mother could want. Whether she would call her back for me. If she would give me a hug. But all I ask her about is the dinner.

"Are you coming to dinner on Thursday?" I force a smile, to nip her scolding in the bud.

"I don't know." She always answers in Spanish as opposed to Catalan. "I'm too old for that stuff. Besides, somehow I always end up singing karaoke, all by myself."

"If you're not going, neither am I." I wink at her and leave her muttering something under her breath as she washes her hands before entering the unit.

I think about the last time I had dinner with my co-workers and I can't help but laugh. Alone in front of my locker, as I change out of my work clothes, I remember them dancing on the bar in a place owned by Vanesa's uncle. The more I try to hold in my laughter the harder it is. We made Pili get up on the bar. I turn to glance behind me. There's no one else around. Here, all alone, laughing like a maniac, I feel like the stupidest person in the world. Who laughs when they're alone? I imagine canned laughter like on television shows, designed to trigger chuckles in the viewer through contagion. Laughter that laughs at me. I close the locker and shake my head. I don't have any reason to laugh, but I would say I've got the right to. And what if it turns out I'm losing my mind? After 9/11 in New York, there was the feeling that comedy was dead, that no one would ever laugh again. The comedians were thrown, the comedy clubs closed and no one knew when they'd open back up. Television hosts literally stopped telling jokes and the general sense was that nothing would ever be the same again. But as the years passed they even started making jokes about 9/11 itself, so gradually the tragedy became part of the entertainment, a simple defence mechanism against the horror, a miserable attempt to survive.

I laugh at the hazy memory of that night, the karaoke duet Marta and I performed, and I feel the ultra-fine line separating that laughter from pain, comedy from tragedy, the semi-peace of this moment with the possible war that will come after the phone call. "Mauro Mother". The bright red 1 like a heart about to burst open. I dial and wait. It's better to do it from here. The hospital functions as a shield against what might happen.

The first words she says are "Pauli, dear, I'm so glad you called." I deduce that no one's died, because of the ridiculous nickname with that *au* she keeps way up high and chirpy, and now my heart starts doing its thing, an intermittent atrial flutter. Electrical activity in the heart. If you touched me now you'd get a shock. Mauro's mother continues on the other end of the line, she wants to know how I am, how I'm handling it, they are devastated. With the holidays coming up, dear, you know. "Hmm" is the most I manage to get out between one sentence and the next. Over the years, the few times we've spoken over the phone I've imagined her as a mythological combination of woman's torso and budgie's green head, half *Melopsittacus undulatus* but with prominent breasts and a slight valgum deformity in the legs, the talons

154

of the feet separated and the knees almost touching. From her beak burbles tragedy and all of a sudden she starts crying, and I don't know how to make it stop.

"Listen…" I say, adopting a protective stance towards her. "Please, Rosa, don't cry. Mauro wouldn't want to see you like this, you hear me?"

I suddenly realized that over these months since his death I must have been repeating something similar to myself, and perhaps that's why I don't cry, but the reflection smacks more of hypothesis than revelation. The nasal sounds coming from Mauro's mother multiply by ten through the phone's shell, her sobs break up into a hailstorm inside the receiver, which I have to pull away from my ear because it hurts. She calms down, apologizes, takes a breath and then comes out with it: "We were thinking that we'd love to have you come over for a little while on Christmas Day."

I see the long sentence written in chalk on a green board and myself, from behind, struggling to diagram it, determine its structure, components and functions. I've never been good with words. It's an algorithm to decode, a trap. I'm lost and I don't even know what is the subject of a predicate that I'm now certain doesn't exist. I close my eyes and sit down on the floor. I can't speak, so she continues with those melodious emissions of characteristic sounds that vary in intensity and potency. Just like budgies, her tone gets more intense, excitable, deafening when she feels in danger. She knows that she's most likely going to get no for an answer. Why does she make herself so vulnerable?

"Thing is, Rosa, I'm going to be out of town until late and I don't want to keep you all up."

They'll wait for me, she says, it's a holiday and they won't be in any rush, they want to see me, she repeats, and she wants to give me all the things that she'd been saving for if we ever got married. And besides, dear, I have something to tell you: my husband has been working on it and even though there was no will there is a small inheritance, and since there are no children and we don't need it, it should go to you. We'll let you know when you need to go in to the solicitor's office. The solicitor's? I say without air. Yes, dear, you have to sign a document. It should go to you. My heart stops. I feel humiliated, weak, defeated, and she won't shut up. Some bedspreads made by a grandmother who knitted, some Bohemian crystal glasses and some money that Mauro had saved up. I hyperventilate. I chew on the inside of my cheeks. It makes no sense. Another name, heiress, a name that makes me very angry with her. She has no right to call me that, she's never respected my wishes, she never listened to what was so hard for me to make clear, what I enunciated like an insistent child, when at Sunday lunches she would get me against the ropes if we ended up alone together in the kitchen, or in front of everyone as she cut the dessert: that there would be no wedding. You should get married, dear, she would say, closing in, and as the knife made its way through the puff pastry, she'd bear down: you're not getting any younger. That opened up my wound, whipped cream emerging like my regret about being there, surrounded by an atmosphere I'd never asked for and a concept of traditional family I didn't want and didn't comprehend. It's a relief to know that Mauro's mother's invasive attitude was an ally in our downfall, it wasn't all my fault. Somehow I manage to take in a wisp of air, enough to articulate the severe words that follow.

"I don't want the money, Rosa. So there's no need for me to sign anything and listen, I'm very sorry, really, but no, I'm not coming on Christmas Day."

Hail in my ear again, she blows her nose, I hear something like "I knew it, I knew you wouldn't want to." Click. She hung up. She hung up on me! I'm about to call her back, flummoxed, to tell her there's no need for us to get angry with one other, but the bedspread comes to mind. A bedspread, she'd said, and crystal glasses. I stop. Don't call her, Paula. For if you ever got married. For years I've been trying to free myself from her whims and my inability to pull that off, even now, when her son is an eternal distance away, feels like a punishment I don't deserve.

Sitting on the floor, I see the dust under the lockers. Grey puffs like tumbleweed on a blustery day. On Thursday I'll go to the dinner and I'll laugh. You hide the dregs of life where you can.

* * * * * *

Marita says—in her coastal Colombian Spanish, with faint
"s"s—that "Sometimes when I iron the clothes in the bedroom I sense Señor Mauro's presence."

Today she arrived with a letter from Social Security in
hand. I don't know why she keeps her nails so badly painted,
in that fuchsia colour. If she just left them bare she could
neglect them as much as her nasty little heart desired, but
she paints them and then, instead of removing the polish
when it gets all chipped, she just leaves it on, as a sign to me
of her privation. You hired her under your name, Mauro.
That has to be changed. She says that "It gives me the willies
to see the señor's name on the letters" and that "It's best to
free the dead of earthly concerns". She still calls you "señor"
and you know as well as I do that she'll never stop. I'm
already sick of telling her that we don't like it, that it makes
us uncomfortable. Now I shift it into the singular, I tell her
that I don't like it, that it makes me uncomfortable, but she
continues just the same, like with those fingernails, her need
to make me feel bad, and mark class differences and distances.
Now what do I do, Mauro? Without your shirts, your meals,
your freakish neatness and order, Marita is an unnecessary
expense, and you know how much she bugs me when I'm
home. She never shuts up. I don't understand that story she

always tells me about a man she loves who's waiting for her in Tubará, in a yucca field, while she cleans all hours of the day to feed those children that sprout up from beneath the rocks. One day you reproached me, saying I look down on her, that Marita's life is like a novel, with a love story out of a novel. She's the one who looks down on me, trust me. But she adored you, and she still does. Were you trying to tell me something with that remark about a love story out of a novel? Maybe that ours wasn't? When did I stop listening to you, stop paying attention to you?

In the beginning you would leave me those notes you were so fond of. "Can you pick up some window cleaner, detergent and bleach? On Friday I'll wash the windows if it doesn't rain, although your father called and said there are storms coming." But I'm almost transparent, I practically live at the hospital, I sleep here, I pass through barely touching the floor, I don't make messes, I don't consume. I'm well stocked with cleaning supplies, I've got them coming out of my ears. Everything is still, Mauro, or perhaps I'm the one who doesn't dare to move even a single leaf. Five hundred grams of green beans don't make a mess and that's become the measure of how exciting my day-to-day life's become.

"Don't you sense him? Right there, next to the clothes in the wardrobe. Don't worry because he is taking care of you."

I could punch her, Mauro. I could take off an espadrille and smack her with it until she shuts up. Do I tell her that you're no longer mine? Does anyone burden the ballerina with the weight of your absence beside *her* wardrobe? But that's not why I'd hit her. I'd hit her until she convinced me one hundred per cent that she could feel you and sense you, so I can be sure she does and isn't just having me on. I don't feel anything. I don't feel you, I don't sense you. I wanted to fire her. I don't need her anymore, can't you see that? And now she comes with her fingernails a mess and her eyes damp to tell me that she senses you beside our wardrobe, and I know for sure that I will go through with the name change and, while I'm at it, I'll give her an open-ended contract, because while she can somehow feel you I'll try my best to feel you, too.

* * * * * *

13

The first new thing about this strange Christmas: we are spending it in Selva de Mar. The idea of driving kilometres and kilometres along a deserted motorway to a seaside town on Christmas Day had me pacing around the flat, dragging my heels, taking slow sips on my coffee and glancing down into it as if expecting it would grant me permission to hide away at home and avoid my father's family.

Christmas is already here, pulling no punches. I have to act like everything's going fine, that there's no one missing at the table, and wait for the holiday to be over, treat it like just another day in the calendar.

As a little girl I would stare, mouth agape, at the normal families on the beach, the complete families. I studied their spontaneity, how they moved in a group, how they talked amongst themselves, how they shouted, all sorts of verbal and non-verbal communication they understood and enacted that was absent in my home. I didn't have that experience of family. I was thrilled by the ruckus that could be raised by the members of a tribe smeared in sunblock, the unmistakable whine of children's shrieks swaddled in the buzz of the waves and the seagulls. Next to my towel was my father's: immaculate, with his newspaper, *La Vanguardia*; his pack of

Marlboros; his notebook with twelve staves and the fountain pen he wouldn't let me even get close enough to sniff. We went there in his brand-new Seat Panda, a small car that still managed to embody a middle-class dream of total freedom. I remember my father's satisfied face as he drove, and my inability to spark up a conversation from the back seat. In our free fall, subjects like the music he composed for advertising, current affairs and how my day had gone at school became the web supporting a routine we'd already grown accustomed to. It was when we broke with our daily rituals, when we had blank spaces, leisurely summers, or at Christmas time or Easter week, that a wall composed of my mother's absence rose between us. On the beach I would shout from the water for him to come play with me, to search for crabs on the rocks and collect clams and shells, but he didn't want to leave our things alone on the sand and asked if we could take turns swimming. I brought him all the shells I could find with a hole in them and asked him to make me a necklace, like the ones Mum used to make for me. To be fair, he tried, but I could see his gaze darkening as he struggled with the fishing line, so I soon stopping asking him for necklaces on the beach. Little by little, I put aside what had been my normality. There would be no more necklaces, that little girl faded away and with her, her mother. Sometimes my aunts would come to spend the day at the beach and indiscreetly point out those two buttons that were already hinting at breasts. My aunts and those startling topics of conversation seemed to be from another planet, they made me jump up, haughty and coated in sand, and distance myself from them as much as I could. I realized that there was a life parallel to the isolation my father and I shared, that the world's heart beat to a quite different rhythm. My relationship with him was different from the relationships my friends had with their fathers. Nobody else's father was a composer. The other fathers were bankers, electricians, salesmen, teachers, but that wasn't what made us so unusual; it was that unexplored void between us, our inability to move beyond the gaping loss. When you're little you perceive many things but lack the strength to change them.

We've grown up and now, in a house in a town overlooking the sea, my father's sisters are trying to determine whether the stuffing in the chicken we ate last night at a friend's house had dried apricots in it or not, and my uncles have all their hopes of winning the league pinned on the return match. I look at my cousins, Anna and Beth, with chubby babies in their arms, immersed in one of those exclusive conversations all first-time mothers feel the need to have with other mums, convinced they're the first to experience some particular aspect of motherhood, while their husbands drink distractedly and try to agree on the music. To my left is my cousin Toni's new girlfriend, who showed up without warning, somebody named Glòria. She's taking a reflexology course underwritten by the municipal government, according to her, for the jobless. Glòria has purple streaks in her hair and curls them around her fingers as she explains to me that the Cherokee have always given great importance to feet.

"For everything, for maintaining physical, mental and spiritual balance. So massage is part of a sacred ceremony because they believe feet are our contact with the earth and the energies that flow through it," she explains, arching her eyebrows very high. "Our spirits are linked to the universe through our feet."

I'm a little bit itchy all over. The verb *flow* has always given me hives and I don't have Mauro next to me, so I can't pinch his thigh to let him know he should save me from this conversation.

There is nothing more depressing than altering the natural course of things. Selva de Mar equals summer. Dad's house equals sandals. The beach umbrella in a corner, the hammock filled with dried leaves, and the radiators on in a house built for opening the windows and letting in the sky and the sun. Nothing makes sense this Christmas, everything's out of place, twisted, uncomfortable and lifeless. My father thinks that by celebrating Christmas here we are breaking with what we've always done in Barcelona and perhaps that way, he says, we can forget that Mauro isn't with us anymore. At least he was able to verbalize it. I think I appreciate that. It makes the reality a little less burdensome.

"Toni told me what happened," says Glòria in a hushed tone, while the others are talking louder and louder. "Please accept my condolences."

How long will I have to hear that bullshit? If only I were capable of telling her that we've just met and I don't want to accept anything from her. I move my lips slightly, a pseudosmile to get past the moment.

When my dad appears holding a clay pot filled with the traditional seafood stew, we applaud. Time passes with the clinking of silverware, laughter and stories that sprout up each year as if they were new. All of a sudden I realize we're using the linen napkins that my mother embroidered with small green leaves, in a dimension I'm convinced is not this one. Four decades later the napkins are bunched up next to the plates and touching new, greasy lips, such as Glòria's, as she dominates the conversation, explaining how she's an expert in the evolutionary tarot.

"Oh, so there's more than one tarot?" my dad asks as he serves the plates.

Aunt Rosalia, Toni and his brand-new girlfriend get into a heated discussion on the difference between divinatory and evolutionary tarot, the fun is in the interpretation of the spreads, the evolutionary deck is better, says Glòria in an expert's voice, because you can help the person break negative energy knots.

This must be a joke, I can't believe this is really happening. My father turns towards me with a sly smile and winks. It's his way of asking me to wait it out, it's better to laugh than to cry. As is often the case in these sorts of gatherings, the conversation topics burn through quickly and before long it seems the cards are forgotten and the talk amongst the women at the table turns to my weight, that I look haggard, I'd be prettier with a few more kilos, I'm too skinny, that working in the health profession I can't go around looking so sickly. My father comes over with the excuse of clearing the table and gets Rosalia's attention, he tells her we're not going through an easy time and his use of the plural, that unexpected paternal display, touches me, to a surprising degree.

When the conversations start up again, Glòria returns to the subject, in a hushed voice.

"I think you could probably benefit from a session. Look, I won't insist, but I think you should know that people who've lost their significant others are more predisposed to communicating through the tarot, you can communicate with him through a message he sends you in dreams," she concludes, bringing the fork into her mouth.

And then I rise up from the chair, dragging it loudly, capturing everyone's attention, which is the last thing I was trying to do today. I'm cruel to the linen napkin, throwing it down on the floor in a rage.

In August I told my dad to have the toilet cistern fixed and I see it's still got a slow but constant drip. From the bathroom I hear them murmuring. Since Mauro's not here I've heard those murmurs a lot. I can easily translate them now. It's like being laid out in hospital in a coma and everyone is talking about you, convinced you can't hear them. But you can, and just their tone is enough for you to know that in their machinations you're a victim, not a heroine. I swallow my bad mood when, sitting there on that toilet, I get a flash of clairvoyance that I've no one else to spend Christmas with and, without wanting to, I project myself into the future and see myself surrounded by these same people one Christmas after the other.

I wash my face, take a deep breath and order myself to calm down. I tell myself that today will soon end, and I leave the toilet with as much dignity as my chagrin allows. When I come back the voices stop and everyone looks at their plates.

"Sorry," I manage to say, and the clink of silverware returns and gradually their voices reach a normal volume.

The conversation around the table after the meal is without incident and luckily the first people to leave are Toni and Glòria. We walk them to the car and everyone goes back inside because it's frightfully cold, but I stay out a little longer, searching for a line of mobile coverage. The memory of Pep inserts itself like a clause, from many kilometres away. I haven't heard from him. Damp air pregnant with the scent of the water and seaweed insists on slipping through my clothes, flooding some sort of well that today seems to fill me up entirely.

I offer to change the nappies on my cousins' daughters. They are gorgeous and radiate an innocence that makes it easy to slip away from the adult world. I carry both the girls off, dividing the weight on my hips. They look at me suspiciously with round mouths and plump lips as I walk, singing softly. Together they are only a few kilos of tender flesh and the scent of baby cologne. I lay them out on my dad's bed and spend a good long while playing with their chubby feet, occasionally glancing at the clock. Today the hours pass slowly. These babies seem enormous compared to mine in the NICU. Two fat, healthy girls who I'll see grow up from one Christmas to the next. Their language of sounds calms me, like the delicate cowlick one of them has at the back of her neck. After a while I reappear in the dining room with the two girls and hand them over to their mothers, who have already started to miss them. Motherhood must be that, I tell myself, constant suffering.

When everyone has left, I clear the table with my dad. I serve myself a little more wine, we could say that this now is Christmas, the smallness of that moment fenced in by the sound of the dining room clock echoing in the emptiness of a house that doesn't understand what's going on today.

The second new thing about this strange Christmas: a father and daughter selfishly protecting their little, impenetrable circle. No one else can understand what the exclusivity of having each other means. It's a brand-new feeling, and at the same time it's as remote as our first Christmas without Mum.

My dad is humming a melody with his brows furrowed, the way he's done ever since I can remember, focused on placing the plates and glasses properly in the dishwasher. I look at him from the kitchen doorway while I savour the glass of wine, one of the many I've had over the course of the day, and for the first time I see an old man, really old, I mean, as if he'd aged suddenly, as if all of a sudden he'd lost what had made it hard to pin a specific age on him. Yet, at the same time, beneath that more vulnerable man, I sense the man who raised me and who, in his way, loves me more than anyone else. I see him blurrily but he's still there, tall and still strong, with that attractive nape of the neck where unbelievably pure white hairs emerge. He looks healthy and wise, with long, slightly bandy legs in beige corduroy, leather belt and coins ringing in his heavy, swollen pockets, the sturdy man who rises early no matter the day, who reads the paper at the bar, loves conversation around the table after meals and is a good friend to his friends, who's always on the edge of his seat about the weather forecast, dramatizing the prospect of a few drops of rain as if it were Noah's flood and turning a hot day into a tragedy, the man forever in love with the memory of a woman, who sits at the piano and opens up the door to a world that is his and only his. That is my dad, and despite everything, he reminds me of someone young wearing an old man costume, his white eyebrows thicker, the wrinkles on his forehead and receding hairline exaggerated, he even rounds his back and makes hesitant motions as he carries kitchen implements to and fro. He moves decisively within his small universe of pots and baskets, and demijohns of olive oil he buys from a lifelong friend who makes and bottles it exclusively on demand. I'm sure that every time they get together he pretends he needs a demijohn just to make his friend happy. I counted six in the pantry alone.

"I'm really sorry about before, Dad. I lost my cool."

He turns with a start.

"I didn't know you were here. Forget about that, Paula. Your cousin… well, don't get me started… he found a woman who fits him to a T."

We both laugh under our breath.

"A fortune teller, just what this family needed."

"Paula, stop it, come on!"

I burst out in a long, hard laugh, as if someone was pushing all the bad out of me, and my dad turns out to be the perfect companion for gathering up the bits and bobs of me that need to be put back together.

"That's quite enough. Leave them alone. They're made for each other!"

He runs a damp dishcloth over the cold marble counter and collects the crumbs and dirt in his hand as we draw out our criticizing and laughing, suddenly in collusion.

The bells of Sant Esteve Church mark six. I have the feeling we are all alone in the world. Me and my dad. Suddenly I get a shiver. I gulp down the rest of my wine.

"I have a present for you," I tell him, with genuine enthusiasm.

"Me first, missy. Sit down on the sofa, please."

He dries his hands with a tea towel that he then puts down by the sink, and walks over to the piano, pulling down his shirt and the sleeves of his jumper, and quickly buttoning the cuffs.

He sits down at the seat of the old piano he rescued years ago from the dump. The yellowed keys harmoniously complement the aged wood. He looks at me and gestures for me to wait. Then he places a score on the music stand and when his fingers are just centimetres from the keys, he stops, picks up the score, and shows it to me.

"It's not called 'Bella' anymore. I changed the name, see?"

I have to grind my teeth and brace my heart to hold back the emotion that invades me when I see my name printed on the very top, crowning rows of staves filled with notes that begin to sound, turning me into a bittersweet melody. He plays with his eyes closed, rocking his head the way he always does and pressing the pedals with those big feet, and suddenly the love I feel for this man chokes me up. My father turned these last few months into music for me, a composition intimately tied to my emotional ups and downs. I'm a little self-conscious that the result is so minimalist and moving, the tender piano melody matches the compassion I've often caught in his gaze when we're having lunch together, when we meet up for a coffee. There's a harmony that closes the piece that he wanted to make hopeful, but I think that, deep down, those notes also speak of everything he's never been able to put into words with me.

There's a brief silence when he ends, before I start clapping, and I stand to hug him. I feel him returning my embrace, I sense how he struggles to make his arms tender, they're like two stiff branches, he encircles me and gives me a few pats on the back. We don't know how to be physically affectionate, there's always been cold stone between us, but then, completely unexpectedly, he pulls away slightly and sits me down on his lap. At first it makes me uncomfortable but I manage to overcome my inevitable shyness at such a physical display of love from him, giving in to it, feeling a rush of memories that take me back to the innocent girl I must have been before the age of seven. I'd sat on his lap before, plenty of times, and we'd played the piano together, but then came the silences, each of us exiled to our own territory, and when we tried to come together again we found that time had changed us. Here, in this improvised nativity scene at the piano, I realize deep down we never entirely lose touch with the child inside us.

"Thank you for coming today. I know it wasn't easy." He blurts it out without looking up from the floor and I don't know what to say. "I wanted to tell you something, but I don't know how."

My heart skips a beat. All the closeness I'd always yearned for now abruptly becomes a burden.

"And that's why you wrote the song?" I ask, my voice hoarse.

"No, no. The song is a gift. My Christmas gift to you. Did you like it?"

I nod, pressing my lips together. And then he closes his eyes and takes my hands between his, the way men of a certain age often do when they're struggling to say something heartfelt.

"What I wanted to tell you… I wanted to tell you that…. give me a moment here. I need to know that you're OK."

"I'm OK, Dad," I hasten to say, burning with embarrassment.

"Paula." He lifts up my face and turns it towards his. "I went through the same thing you're going through now."

"It's not exactly the same, Dad."

He looks at me with surprise. He notices an unexpected elusiveness in my tone. I don't need him dragging me towards that desperation he swathed himself in when Mum died, where he held me, stuck, as a spectator, a seven-year-old insect trapped on the hairy leaf of a carnivorous plant. They had a good marriage. A daughter, plans for a future together that justified—to a certain extent—that anxious silence we were plunged into without her. I need to tell him that Mauro didn't want me anymore, that there's no post mortem status for the person left behind in those conditions. I have to stress that my intention is to get past this, not turn Mauro's death into doctrine the way he did with my mother's.

"But I know how you're feeling, Paula."

"No, you don't," I insist.

"You loved him very much. You loved each other very much."

He inhales audibly, fighting back the emotion that memory evokes.

"Besides…" I change the subject and try to invert our roles with an insinuation, "you were by Mum's side up until the last second. But I had lunch with Mauro the day he died, and you know what?" He looks at me and shrugs as if nothing could surprise him. "We argued, in fact he told me that…"

I look around nervously. He is radiating the same misplaced emotion as everyone else, and the temptation to tell him that Mauro was with another woman draws me like a magnet. I need to say it and for him to understand all my pain, I need to rub up against his chest, against his legs, in search of his compassion, rub up hard against him like a cat seeking protection and affection.

I catch the poisoned thought in time, perhaps out of fear of hurting the old man I was surprised to see a little earlier in the kitchen. What would be the point of snatching away his idea of a son-in-law now?

"What did he tell you?"

"Nothing, nothing important. We argued and he had to leave, to go to a meeting at work. I didn't want to hug him goodbye, Dad. That's how things were."

I release a sigh filled with resentment but maintain my smile like a load-bearing wall. I stroke a key without meaning to and a tragic A slips out. He rubs my back. He says I shouldn't think about that now, that there's no point. We embrace. It's a strange moment. Death is the great choreographer of strange moments stuffed into awkwardly timed conversations.

"What I mean is, don't feel bad about rebuilding your life, for having fun from now on. I mean that's exactly what you have to do. Life is made up of pieces, of phases, and Mauro is just one piece of your life. One piece with its ups and downs, but a lovely piece nevertheless. Whatever it was you argued about, it'll never be as messed up as his death, and bitterness, sweetie, well, it's useless. Completely useless, trust me."

And as I'm thinking how I missed my chance to demand he react like a warrior dad, defend my dignity with sword and shield and not let anyone walk all over his daughter, he disarms me with a kiss on my forehead that arrives decades too late, but still, it arrives.

At the very least we must make a curious sight. A forty-two-year-old woman, with her head bowed stifling both tears and truths, on the lap of a seventy-two-year-old man making a visceral display of sincerity in front of a piano that gives off a scent of firewood, holding hands, the atmosphere imbued with an awkward timidity.

"These things dissolve, they're not that exceptional, you know? They're enormous when they happen but then they shrink and dissolve. Move forward. You have to live, Paula. Promise me you will?"

The third new thing about this strange Christmas: my dad is here for me, he always has been, and he knows things about me that I could never have guessed. Love is tangible, audible and brave. The requirement for feeling it is as simple as being there. I promise him.

* * * * * *

When someone dies, their friends are reallocated. I got Nacho.

You have to see him with the twins. He showed up this morning in Plaça de la Virreina looking like a one-man band, loaded way up high with bags and gadgets and a double pushchair unsuited to the narrow streets of Gràcia, where he and Montse insist on living. The tension between me and Nacho, since that day at the hospital, is all your fault.

"You're hitting it pretty hard, eh?"

He nodded at my glass. I made a gesture to say he should let it go and not ask questions. It's your fault I drink wine at eleven thirty in the morning, too. I needed that wine to screw up my courage, to tell him that I wish he'd told me that you were with somebody new, but deep down I get that he was your friend and I respect his loyalty, so in the end I kept my accusations to myself. The truth is I even held his hand when he said that stuff about how he misses you all the time. It's hard to have a conversation with two babies moving around, calling into question the gravity of our situation. More than once I'd been left alone at the table, first because he had to change a nappy, and then because the other one was having a tantrum. They would put things they shouldn't into their mouths and try to twist their little bodies out of the pushchair.

Nacho was working like a dog and apologizing to everyone at the bar. In a moment of peace he told me that the feeling of not hearing anything from you, of knowing that you would never come back, had hit him so hard that he'd even made an appointment with a psychologist, and I looked at his cracked lips and fragile expression and I understood that if you hadn't left me, without the filter of knowing there was someone else in your life, the horror would have filled my days with endless suffering. I felt my heart shrink with guilt. And all of a sudden, amid the ruckus of the two little ones, the noise of a dragging chair nearby, the slam of a cupboard door and the whistle of the coffee machine on the bar, I heard myself saying that missing you so much is the proof that we love you, Mauro, and that no one can fill the place you occupied in our lives.

Outside, I kissed the twins goodbye, although they pulled away from my display of affection, and then Nacho and I spontaneously came together in a warm hug we both needed, and I walked home alone, in silence, along streets still ringing with Christmas joy.

* * * * * *

1 4

When I woke up I didn't know where I was, I was completely
disoriented. My shift seemed calm, so I'd stretched out on one
of the beds that was empty because Marta and Vanesa were
taking a break on the bunk beds. I observed them without
taking part in their conversation. They almost always wore
the same hairstyle. Long and straightened, with a similar
fade of chestnut and blonde tones and a diagonal fringe with
overly made-up eyes peeking through. Pearl earrings that
don't give off the pure light of real pearls. Marta also has
more than one piercing in her upper ear, a small attempt
to make it clear she's the one holding the reins of her life.
Vanesa radiates more innocence, and sometimes, despite
their professionalism and how much I like them, I feel like
they don't fit in. I know they both loved watching TV shows
set in hospitals like most people of their generation, and
even though I've never asked them, I sometimes imagine
that it was fiction that compelled them along a university
path leading to a real set that may not be exactly what
they'd been dreaming of. Here blood's coagulating and lives
are in real danger. Yet I notice they have identical hairdos
and wear too much make-up, that the presence of young
male medical staff makes them repeat certain gestures too
frequently.

Anaesthetized in their moment, they talked and fiddled with their phones, revealing the last flash of the teenagers they must have been not so many years ago. They had that attitude some young people have, thinking the world owes them everything just because they have to work; Marta was furious because she wasn't originally scheduled for a shift that night, she'd been called in and then, because of some last-minute changes, all three of us were there, which was more staff than strictly necessary. I was fine with that. I always think of it as serving a purpose much larger than myself, but she saw it as some sort of punishment because it interrupted her Christmas holidays. Vanesa was taking her side, using all those understanding, sympathetic words I can't stand. The room was thick with their resignation, impotence, and most of all indifference to their responsibilities, making it seem as if they were the victims.

To break with the bad undercurrent, I tried to strike up a conversation, first talking about the strange calm on that penultimate night of the year; when I got no response, I asked them if they were cold. I was freezing and pointed out that the radiator wasn't turned on.

"I'm fine, Paula," said Vanesa, but Marta kept gnawing on a hangnail with her gaze lost in the distance.

I decided to turn on the radiator and leave them alone. I took off the top of my uniform so I wouldn't smell like hospital and I curled up with the scent of fabric softener from my jumper. It was the next best thing to being under my sheets at home. After a little while they started to speak in a soft voice about what they were going to wear the next day to a New Year's Eve party, discussing whether the black top one of them had lent the other would look good with some trousers they'd bought.

The possibilities of a party seemed so remote to me and all of a sudden I felt such longing. I'd been there, here, with that urge and the smell of tobacco in my clothes hours after leaving the club, heading straight to work after a night out partying. I remember myself then, with my head held high and a bespoke confidence I'd constructed in familiar territory. I was in control of situations at home, and at the hospital I knew to smile, I liked my friends. What can I do to mend all that now?

During the last few months I'd lost track of the calendar. It was only overheard snippets of other people's conversations, like their talk of that New Year's Eve party, that made me aware of how much time had passed since the accident the previous February. But that night, stretched out and tired, with Marta and Vanesa close by, I was intensely aware of how many hours were left in the year, I heard them drop, one after the other, in a countdown narrated by Pep's distant voice on the other end of the phone line. The next day, 31 December, was the day he was scheduled to arrive in Barcelona, or at least that's what he'd told me. I had been waiting to hear from him since the call I'd made a little more than a month before, but his silence made me think that maybe I'd dreamt it. Deep down, I trusted he'd be calling any minute to let me know he'd landed. Again the insidious nerves, I can't play them off, not at work and not even alone with myself, unable to concentrate on a single thing as the month draws to a close, as if he held the solution to my soporific life and was bringing it from Boston. The hope of seeing him pushed me through Christmas and the invasion of friends who'd flooded in to spend time with me during the holidays, to diffuse the harshness we are all feeling over accepting that Mauro's gone. But the ache only grew with their insistence, reinforcing the image of what we'd been in the past, not just Mauro and me as a couple but all of us as a group.

Over the last few years I've moved between three different groups of friends, all small, compact and consistent. Lídia, my closest colleagues at work, and the group of friends I shared with Mauro. Now that last group makes me uncomfortable. They're all couples and surrounded by children. I've been branded a singleton. On the other hand, Mauro's death turned them into a powerful army, an army willing to march forward to grab me and make me their hostage. Death's tentacles are long and indiscreet, they slip without permission into relationships, making them fragile and brittle.

I tried to welcome them into my home, have food, treats and drinks ready, follow their conversations, bear the weight of other people's happiness and the forced joy of Christmas. I was affectionate and returned their generosity with thoughtful details and effort. It seemed they stayed forever, their good intentions diluting over the hours into an ephemeral form of kindliness. As if it were a normal Christmas, I forced myself to buy a little gift for all the children in the group, some dummy holders covered in different fabrics from a small neighbourhood shop. As I was buying them and the salesgirl was showing me all the fabrics, I felt like myself and was happy with the prospect of gift-giving; later, at home, I wanted to wrap them in personalized packages like I'd seen on the internet. But the charm of the wrapping was in the ribbons, and I couldn't place them or knot them correctly; my ineptitude at crafts that I'd always readily accepted became instead an infuriating hodgepodge of nerves. I balled up the paper. I was discovering that impotence, pain and sadness don't lessen over time, just transform into a tenuous, fickle state. All I can do is pretend. I've become a recalcitrant actress, methodically building a career that will lead me straight to an Oscar. Sometimes I pull off a masterful performance, doing it so well I can scarcely believe it myself, until some insubordinate ribbon sends me into a rage and I'm slamming little boxes filled with dummies and the happiness of others against the bedroom wall.

So, waiting for signs of life from Pep has got me through the first Christmas without Mauro. The two nights before my shift I slept very badly. I would wake up and check my phone in the small hours and, as I forced myself to go back to sleep, I recreated possible reunion scenes with Pep. Would we embrace dramatically? Would we keep a few feet between us waiting for the other to break the ice? With my head beneath the pillow, the recriminations would alight; I told myself not to think about him, that if he wanted to see me again he would have made some indication, maybe wishing me a happy Christmas. It's true that I hadn't either. I didn't even know what he was doing in Boston, I only knew a few details about his life and everything seemed to indicate that he was into freedom, fun and wringing the last drops out of every day. The odds that he would even come back, much less that we'd go off together somewhere, were very slim.

The voices of the two junior doctors as they discussed their expectations for that New Year's Eve party rocked me into a sound sleep. During night shifts, when there isn't a lot going on, I often stretch out for a few hours and doze off, but I'd never slept that deeply before. I'd never been so tired either, so exhausted from paying so much attention to myself.

I'd been asleep for maybe two hours when my pager went off. Cardiac arrest in room 125. I woke up alone and frightened with my sleepiness printed all over me. I put on my white coat and ran to the stairs, mechanically, as I had so many times before. I heard the distant creaking of doors and the halls lengthened as I walked. When I got to 125 there were already medical staff there, and I didn't see the baby in the crib. I looked on the sofa, on the mother's empty bed, nothing. The baby wasn't there.

"Where's the baby?" I knelt down and placed my face against the cold linoleum floor to look for her under the sofa.

"Paula." Marta knelt beside me and touched my shoulder. Then she spoke very softly, so that the others wouldn't hear. "It's the grandmother, the baby is fine, she's with her mother in the nursing room. It was the grandmother who went into cardiac arrest."

"What?" It took me a little while to get my bearings and realize that, on the other side of the bed, there was an elderly woman laid out on the floor while Vanesa and a doctor attended to her. My embarrassment filled me with a sudden warmth. The doctor glanced at me sidelong when I came over and a few minutes later, when everything was under control and they'd carried the woman out on a stretcher, I thought he was talking about me, pointing to the sofa and laughing under his breath. I knew that when he explained the anecdote to the whole team coming in fresh, early in the morning, I would even laugh myself. I knew that the comic image of a doctor looking for a baby underneath a sofa would have a long shelf life and be the raw material of jokes; I'd probably even tell some myself, but at that moment I wanted to scream into that doctor's face that being this groggy was just the tip of the iceberg of bedlam. It's so hard for us to be aware of others' pain, to imagine how far the ice extends beneath the water's surface.

At eight in the morning we did the shift change. When we'd finished, the anecdote came up and we laughed at the odd searching I'd done in room 125 a few hours earlier. We were all there: Santi and the other two neonatologists on the team; Marta, who no longer seemed so annoyed; Vanesa; and the secretary, a shy, pink-coloured girl who was equal parts efficient and fearful. Leaning against the wall, they listened to me and joked, some with their hands in the pockets of their lab coats, others holding cups of coffee. Santi had tousled my hair. I liked that feeling of being part of a team, of being loved.

I went through the service exit clinging to that warmth, pushing the door, exhausted, my features fallen, my hair a mess and my eyes gleaming. The daytime world was just waking up with the usual sounds of the outpatient lobby, which was calm at that time of the morning: men and women in white lab coats, a father chasing after a feverish toddler and the cleaners mopping up the emergencies of the night before, the first light of day burnishing the space in preparation for the next batch of patients.

31 December. As soon as I leave the lobby, cold air slaps my face like a warning and I fight with my hair, tangled bizarrely by a sudden wind. I was looking for the car keys in my purse, cursing my habit of always putting them in the little inner pocket that zips shut. My wool gloves were complicating the procedure significantly. Before leaving I'd checked my phone screen, my hopes already dashed, and all I'd found was the message my dad had sent me at 7 a.m. to let me know that the north wind was blowing very hard in Selva de Mar and to please be careful, because despite the calm sky in Barcelona there was an alert for strong gusts. The world, however, continued to spin on its axis. Or at least that's what I thought.

"Dr Cid!"

I looked up and pulled back the hair blowing into my face so I could see clearly. Standing there in trainers, with a long open coat that fluttered like a cape, his hands in his pockets, his shoulders relaxed and his neck tilted slightly back, expectantly, was Pep, devilish as ever.

I stopped short. In the seconds after I heard him call out my name I had a cautious feeling of triumph. He'd come. I had won, and the shadow and its long string of reproaches had lost.

"Pep…"

Naming him in a whisper to retain him, to make sure it was true for just an instant, and then noticing I was short of breath. My heart beating enthusiastically, and the more rational part of me ordering me to slow it down by any means necessary.

The distance of almost a year had given me the space to reinvent him with fake details: he didn't have that many grey hairs before; he was taller than I'd remembered, and he had a more imposing presence. He had a small, childlike nose, and lips that were reminiscent of the ribs of a boat. His lively, restless eyes showed no traces of rancour as they studied my reaction impatiently. He was there, he was really there, unexpected, clearly defined, real, like a sharp photograph, no filters.

"How did you know I was here?"

They weren't even close to the first words I'd rehearsed saying to him during my nights of insomnia. "How did you know I was here," not even a sad little hello. I couldn't control my tone because all my efforts were on not letting him get away, not finding myself alone again.

"I couldn't think of any other place to look for you," he said without the slightest irony, and then a little bit of steam emerged from his mouth and I was reminded of Amsterdam and I gripped my stomach with the vertigo that comes with a new affair.

"Hello," I said in a voice oozing with good humour.

We smiled and kissed each other on both cheeks. And then came his masculine scent of cedar, of wood and of musk, travelling straight to my amygdala and hippocampus, irreversibly imprinting on the neural regions that govern emotion and memory.

We recommend mothers sleep with a piece of cloth up against their skin and then place it inside the incubator very close to their babies, so they can breathe in her scent and feel she's nearby, to strengthen the bonds of affection. How could I have been denying my need for that bond with this carpenter who's practically a stranger but pulls me towards him like a magnet, how had I renounced his skin for a year? Paralysed in that gesture of recognition, I wanted to ignore the fact that he knew nothing about what had happened.

"I'm very glad you came."

I squeezed his hand and with the other I held back my hair, in an attempt to deflect the wind that seemed to be celebrating our reunion with a frenzied dance that made the leaves whirl and leap at our feet.

In the car we looked at each other without knowing what to say. It was strange and charming at the same time, and when we reached the ring roads and stopped in traffic, he put his hand over mine as I shifted gears, accompanying me in the gesture of putting the car into first. He kept it there the whole way.

"Do you know what happened to me at the hospital last night?"

He moved so he could see me better, ready to listen. A few hours before the end of that warped year, I existed for someone inside a car on my way home, I was visible, someone was listening to me, and it was a comfort to find myself whole again.

That was when I knew that I would lie to him, maintain that fiction, not reveal the gravity and weight of death that I carried.

The road that leads to Boscana Valley is winding and shady. It's been almost an hour since I left Barcelona, I don't move with ease outside the city and I'm feeling a little dizzy. It makes me nervous not knowing where I am and the GPS seems to have gone crazy since I left the last town behind. The big rock bellies stick out more and more over the side of the road and I can't shake a feeling that danger waits around every bend. I find it strange to take this unfamiliar route with the previous night's unreal physicality still so close to the surface.

"I'll expect you tomorrow."

Pep left me his address jotted on a piece of paper on top of the console table in the hallway.

Coming back from the hospital, we tried to say goodbye in front of my building, still in the car, we kept leaving our sentences hanging unfinished in the air, not really knowing what direction to take. Pep provoked a different energy in me, an intrepid impulse that made me invite him up without thinking too much about it.

We slept for four hours during the day, he blamed it on jet lag and I blamed something like resurrection. In between stretches of sleep there was sex, coffee, a few grams of unexpected normality and an attempt by me to apologize that was cut short by his index finger.

"Whatever it is, we'll have time to talk about it later. You're exhausted and so am I." He pushed a lock of hair out of my face. "I'm spending New Year's Eve with some friends, if you want to join us. They don't live far from here. I'd love it if you came."

"Oh… I already have plans."

I had turned down two or three offers for New Year's Eve. I'd told them all that I was working but, really, the only plan I had was visualizing Pep in Barcelona, seeing him disembark from the plane and typing in my number, keeping that gap in my agenda just in case. And now I was backing out and I surprised myself by saying no, I couldn't spend New Year's Eve with him. This new tendency of recent months worried me, the habit of postponing everything, of plotting out a shield of lies to protect the solitude I felt I both needed and needed to censure.

He shrugged and pulled a comically disappointed face, but I had already seen the low blow reflected in his gaze.

"Your loss, doctor. I have a second proposal. Tomorrow, when your hangover is gone, why don't you grab a small suitcase, fill it up with warm clothes and hiking boots and come spend a couple of days with me?"

"A very seductive offer. I'll think about it. And what are you going to do now?"

"Now? Go home, sleep a little, unpack and go buy some food in case you decide to accept my proposal."

"Stay."

He shot me a naughty look.

"Sleep here for a while. I know it sounds strange, but I'd love it if you did."

"Do you snore?"

I laughed, showing all my teeth.

"Do you?"

"A little, but gracefully."

In the bedroom, the half-lowered blinds played with the sun, drawing a spider web of light and shade. He commented on a painting by Coco Dávez that rested on the parquet.

"It was a gift." As the words came out, I felt a burning sensation scatter across my diaphragm like a fire spreading along petrol-soaked ground. It was acrylic on paper, an indigo blue background with four red strokes insinuating a knot. Mauro had given it to me when I turned forty. The flames continued, moving in a chain reaction to lick the photograph of Midsummer Eve on the table by the bed, and spreading out to the terrace, which had become a desert, the failed battleground of my attempt to resuscitate Mauro's plants. But the fire was focused on the bed itself. Only Mauro and I had slept in that bed, and Lídia's daughters for the occasional nap when they were little. Deconsecrating the altar of the bed. That must be a step. Giving it new uses, allowing Pep into it and yearning for the cedar scent of his skin to impregnate the pillowcases, sheets and every nook of a space that was already beginning to smell of neglect.

He glanced at the photograph out of the corner of his eye when we sat down on the bed, but he didn't say anything.

The art of lying requires concentration and I can't allow myself to weaken over a few objects from my past.

"Do you mind if I take off my shoes?"

"My sleeping invitation is the full package, you can take it all off."

We curled up under the duvet in just our underwear.

"Oh, the treachery! Your feet are freezing! I didn't remember you had ice cubes for feet!"

And amid laughter, the soft down on his arms and hands, and bright banter, we remained facing each other and I closed my eyes so I wouldn't have to face a truth that throbbed insistently at the hidden depths of everything: Pep's body filling Mauro's side of the bed. A man desired but not loved, a new man and one who is no longer there. A man with an easy laugh. A bluff in the shape of a man, and I knew it.

He studied my eyes, searching for my approval. I had him so close and yet it was still so unreal, that sudden happiness. I touched his hair. I kissed his eyelids.

I didn't want a New Year's Eve party, I wanted the precise affection of a friend, the warmth, to sleep and turn off all the voices in my head. I recognized how awkwardly his body fit into mine, but I felt filled with confidence. We made love for a long time and I acted as if it was all completely normal, him licking me, him pushing my arms back roughly, him separating my legs assertively, and I let him do his thing, he didn't give me the option of taking the initiative and I was fine with that, I was fine with it all, being body, flesh, desire, and nothing more. I wasn't set aflame, I couldn't feel the heat, I was too focused on something better: feeling alive and desired.

When we had finished I turned my back to him and came up against the photograph where someone had immortalized Mauro and me laughing, surrounded by the atmosphere on the shortest night of the year, unaware even of the camera's presence. The photo is proof that Midsummer Eve existed, that Mauro existed, and that at some point we had been at peace with each other. It happened and we were happy. I rested my gaze on the only remaining evidence of that.

Pep placed a hand on my hip.

"Paula…"

"Hmm?"

"You've lost a lot of weight."

I should have told him then, I could have reduced the loss and pain to a short, objective sentence, I could have said something like "my best friend, the man who was my partner, died in an accident. But before he did, he left me for another woman. It's been a rough year". But I let him think whatever he wanted to. I was sure he wouldn't imagine a sudden death, and every other response was preferable to that noxious, awkward pity. I took in a breath and released it with a loud sigh.

"Now that you mention it, I might have. I'll have to come and taste everything you learnt to cook in Boston, see if you're really as good as you claim."

Silence. Lungs working deliberately, matching the rhythms of relaxed breathing, the wind outside whistling, wanting to alert me to something. Don't think, Paula. Sleep.

"So, you'll come tomorrow?"

"Yes, I'll come tomorrow."

The road is gorgeous, the shoulders on either side lead into forest thick with oaks and holm oaks. I pull over to call Pep and tell him I think I'm lost but there's no service and the only other people there are a family with kids stretching their legs and they've never heard of the valley, so I keep going forwards, the only direction available, towards kilometre fourteen as indicated on the wrinkled paper, and after extending my neck to see the end of an endless bend, a discreet sign on one side welcomes me to the national park I believe the valley is in. Seeing it sends a wave of relief through me, and then I feel pure joy at having got this far.

The sand road snakes through trees and reveals a gentle crest with a farmhouse in the distance, stretches of vines dressed for winter, and rosemary and heather everywhere, still flowerless.

The gravel crunches under the car's tyres when I park in front of a stone house that must be his because I haven't seen any others. It's right at the fork in the road, as Pep drew on the map he gave me yesterday. I turn off the engine and get out of the car. The silence is broken only by distant barking and the rustle of the wind through the bare branches of poplars around the house that signal the forest that begins right behind it. Before my eyes can take in all the beauty of the surroundings, the door opens and Pep rushes out to welcome me.

"Come in! You can drive right in!" he shouts from a small porch.

But I leave the car where it is and dart over to him with all the anxious energy of the trip. My legs are trembling. He doesn't understand what a big deal it is that I asked for four days off from the hospital, called up Santi at night and wished him a happy new year and then lied saying fine, he was right, I needed to stop. To pretend I'm a chastened good girl and keep my desire to flee from coming through in my voice. It's a physical desire, impossible to stifle, the same desire that compelled me to quickly pack a suitcase, rescue my least functional underwear from the back of the drawer, look myself in the mirror and practise smiling, rehearse lowering my eyes and emptying all trauma from the depths of my pupils. No, without knowing the whole truth he can't understand or grasp that I've heroically travelled through time to be here today and to be myself, not that other woman who staggers through the shadows. I can't think about her now because that would turn her into a victim and I'd feel bad about marginalizing her. Keeping her silent is closing a chapter and having the courage to leave her past behind, and I love that past, I love it the way you love the darkest, most secret things.

"Hey, doctor… everything OK?"

"Everything is perfectly fine."

I turn to observe my surroundings. Take in a breath. I'm in a small stone house in the middle of a lush forest. A river skirts it like the bow on this surprise gift. I've seen it hundreds of times in fairy tales, the stories with wolves and red hoods, and the prospect of spending the night there is thrilling.

"Welcome to my home."

He has me bundle up and gives me an enthusiastic tour. He's been letting the place for three years. Before that it was the home of some tenant farmers who moved into the town only a ten-minute drive away, he says, pointing to the road. They allowed him to renovate a little and turn a shed into his workshop. We go inside and I sense he's somewhat nervous when the three fluorescent ceiling lights flicker on to reveal a work table covered in blueprints, compasses and all sorts of tools I couldn't name. To the back are a few pieces of furniture and a machine I'd call a chainsaw, that's the best I can do. It smells of wood, resin, glue and varnish.

I run my hand over the back of a dresser that's in the middle of the room.

"Be careful, don't get a splinter. I still have to sand it down."

He puts his hands in his pockets and looks around proudly.

I pick up a tool from on top of a metal filing cabinet.

"This is the first time I've been in a carpenter's workshop."

I stroke the handle that holds a steel blade.

"There's a first time for everything."

I nod and smile.

"What's this called?"

"A gouge. For cutting. Come here, look."

He takes it from my hands and sinks it into a square piece of wood. He shows me a precise cut on the surface, blows the furrow to get rid of the sawdust and then places the tip of my index finger there. It fits perfectly.

Now I understand that Pep belongs in this space, now I see that clearly. The man I could only sense and have been imagining all this time appears before me like an unexpected clearing, and my heart warns me about something but I banish the thought, I need to believe that I can be here, that it's OK to be here today.

I hit bottom, he comments, and I remain silent to obstinately keep the promise I made to myself. His sincerity cannot alter my lie. He told me a year ago that he was divorced, I gave him no details about my life and he didn't ask, so relax, Paula, you don't have to give him any now, either. He quit the consulting office where he worked, tired of the grey, stress-laden atmosphere.

"I used to say that one day I would hang it all up and go to the mountains and raise a few pigs. I don't know how, but I pulled it off."

"You have pigs?" I ask, bewildered.

The question makes him laugh long and hard, a contagious laughter with the ability to transmogrify into a damp kiss that opens a thousand doors and jettisons any chance of backing out.

"No, doctor, I don't have pigs."

He traces my eyebrow with a finger as he looks at me as if for the first time.

"Pep, I… I'm really sorry that I asked you that before, to stay away. I must have seemed rude and you can't have understood why."

"Very rude." He smiles.

"Do you forgive me?" I ask in a thin voice.

He doesn't answer immediately. In fact he even closes his eyes for a moment. I don't know what images he has stored there inside, what information he's searching for; I have no idea what he's revisiting, what he's doing, if he's pulling my leg, what he tells himself, what he thinks, what he's running from or to, if my body is enough for him and he has no interest in my words, maybe he's making a wish, or just clinging to the meaning of my apology. My heart is beating so hard that I'm afraid something will happen to it. My cheeks burn with shame, aware that my speech lacks the key phrase crowned by a black word that can put paid to the magic of every fairy tale.

I don't know him well enough yet, all I know is that he's a simple man, strong and fun, that his vocabulary contains treasures such as *gouge*, that we've been together in this strange way for forty-eight hours and he isn't questioning me, a man who came out of nowhere, like opportunities or those ropes thrown out so you can grab a hold and keep from drowning. I also know that a lie isn't the way to start out on a good footing. Ultimately, I think, a lie is a way to make certain things invisible, and if there's nothing to see, at the very least it undermines death's authority.

"If you help me clean and chop the vegetables I won't hold it against you," he finally murmurs into my ear. But at the same time he takes my hand and squeezes it firmly, in a gesture that belies the frivolity of his joke.

And all of a sudden my mouth is filled with new tastes: fennel, sun-dried tomatoes, aromatic oil, figs. My hands are dusted with flour and I'm flooded with childlike joy as I knead the dough, only pausing the repetitive arm movement I've just learnt to listen to stories about a kitchen that functions as the epicentre of Pep's life. It's far from a mere fuelling station. During the day the sun comes in through its large windows and tiny particles dance anxiously, waiting for him to lift the curtain and turn on the burners of his stage, and when night falls he dines with friends around an enormous, gorgeous table that, of course, he made with his own hands. Sometimes his students sit around it as well, students from a course he teaches with a good friend from Italy who lives in Boston. Giovanna. He pronounces her name playfully trilling the double "n" and it seems his mind travels a little, Giovanna. I wonder but don't ask, and the strangest part is that I don't feel the slightest bit ruffled inside, either. First he tells me that the cooking school belongs to her and is based in Boston, where she lives, that he teaches there when he can, when his woodworking jobs slow down and he has the time and the money, he heads to Boston and stays for a while. For the last few years he's been taking life as it comes and not thinking much about the future. He also hand-crafted the wooden island where he works, where he chops and slices at frightening speed, where he cubes beef, and where he ploughed into me last night and licked me until I lost track of my senses.

There is also the wine that stains burgundy circles on the wood, marking the passing hours, small watery shapes he then wipes with the tea towel always hanging from his waist, off the belt of the Japanese apron that's tied behind him. He makes a gesture of remembering to stir, while still talking, wipes his hands and at the same time grabs me by the waist to move me slightly to the left so he can reach the salt. Here, the wine is like air and again becomes a drink of sweetening, freeing, celebrating, it is no longer the narrow alleyway I fled down just a few days ago. He has me take small sips and teaches me to find its high-intensity aromas, to appreciate its notes of *sous bois*, humus, leather.

"Close your eyes. Don't you get a deep note of ripe blackberry?"

I shake my head.

"Explain it again."

I take another sip and seek out his warm lips, his tongue drenched in wine. Behind us the slow flames caramelize onions and toast a handful of garlic cloves, his hands beneath my woollen jersey, heat on my skin, touch, life at last.

I could remain within this ordinary space and believe that things work this way, like a pause between the first and last acts of life. Why not? It's happening to me, it's as real as the mountains surrounding the valley that indiscreetly observe us, like my hunger that's weakly returned from a distant battle, like last night's clear laughter muffled beneath the blankets and sheets, but the shadow is spying on me from the doorway. It approaches me, stealthy and vigilant.

"Lying is cowardly," it says circumspectly.

It moves away, disappearing into the steam from the pot, but I don't care. Pep has already started taking off my clothes again, and I let him taste the tips of my fingers. I grab him by the arse, we noisily push aside a bowl filled with dates and a handful of walnuts, and he enters me again and again; I put up a provisional wall painful memories cannot slip through, a parenthesis filled with pleasure, caresses, compliments, tickles, these kisses, nothing more than what's in this moment. The logs crackle in the chimney and it is everything.

The next morning we go into town, which is almost completely deserted except for the cats that wander through, their motion contrasting with the silence. Pep explains there's more life there in the summer but that it doesn't change much. Our footsteps echo through the narrow streets. All the town's businesses are concentrated around the town's only square: a newspaper stand, two bars, a butcher's, a supermarket, and two bakeries with their competing tray bakes. In the summer a tiny fishmonger's is open too. There is a small crumbling church with varnished tiles covering the whole roof. We head to the bench a little further up. While Pep runs an errand I wait outside. I couldn't live here. The stillness at the heart of the town makes me anxious and I feel myself getting edgy. What the hell am I doing here? I decide to ring Lídia but at the last minute something stops me and I just send a text saying I'm with Pep, that everything's going really well, that I'm happier than I've been in a long time, that next week we can meet at the hospital and catch up. Texting saves me from having to explain why I haven't said anything until now and from having to put words to this vague state that's taken hold of me like an impertinent memory of something I'm only beginning to glimpse. Every time I notice it I shake my head involuntarily like someone swatting away a pesky fly.

"All done, doctor. Coffee?"

The town square really is pleasant. We combat the cold at our outside table by sitting close to the heaters with our legs crossed; it's good to face the sun and gather up its energy.

"How are you?"

He gently kicks my shoe. My sunglasses quickly become allies. Perhaps the lie has made me paranoid, but I'd say that, every once in a while, Pep is trying to root out information from me.

"I'm feeling very rested but my body's pretty beat up. Curious, isn't it? Oh, and very well nourished. I've got reserves to last me until next January, so you can rest easy."

He smiles reluctantly because that's not what he wants to know. And he takes another stab.

"I like having you in my house. I mean, I'm really glad you could stay for three days, in the end." He leans over and gives me a peck on the lips. Those gestures in the light of day throw me off balance and fill me with an almost

203

infantile shame. "You know, I've thought about you a lot this past year."

The waiter comes with the coffees right then and asks who the black coffee is for and who the white coffee is for and explains something about the temperature of the milk that leaves Pep's words hanging in the air, while I plot how to be sincere without being entirely sincere. The waiter leaves and I manage to gather my composure.

"And what were you thinking?"

"That the times we saw each other and the few conversations we've had made me feel really good. I didn't want to insist, or be a nuisance, I invented all sorts of scenarios for what was going on with you or if I said or did something that upset you. I was dying to see you again. I had to make an effort to not think about you. And you know how it is… the harder you try not to do something, the more you do it."

"I really wanted to see you again too." I stop for a moment and put my sunglasses up on my head so he can see my sincerity. "I appreciate you respecting my silence. I really wanted to be with you, I swear."

"But?"

"I don't know." I shrug and lower my sunglasses again. "I guess we're adults, Pep. Getting involved with someone raises doubts, at least for me. I worry about making a mistake."

"And what are we doing now?"

"Cover in flour and knead well. Preheat oven to two hundred and fifty degrees," I reply glibly, and pat his hand. He throws a balled-up napkin at me.

And that's when it happens. A hearse approaches along the main street. Suddenly it seems as if everything is moving in slow motion. Two pigeons swoop down, flapping frenetically. *Columba livia*, Spanish Barb variety, with big square heads and intense red wattling around the eyes. I'm eaten up by anguish. The church bells toll slowly, the metallic black of the hearse eclipses the scene. The two elderly women dressed in black talking on the corner turn to watch it pass and say something to each other that I can't hear because they cover their mouths with their hands, keeping their prying eyes on the vehicle. A few seconds later, it passes by us and I can see the wreath of flowers tied to the back. A white satin ribbon hangs from it, reading "Always in your children's hearts". I won't fall for that trap, death can't follow me like this. I repeat to myself that it's just a coincidence and that, since Mauro's no longer here, any reminder of death dredges him up. I can control my shaking and this crushing feeling in my chest. You have to control them, Paula, breathe. Lots of people die every day. You should know that better than anyone. Yet, still, a shiver runs up my spine.

"It's a woman." Pep's voice brings me back to the square.

"What?"

"The one who kicked the bucket. It's a woman." He says it in a blatantly indifferent singsong voice as he stirs his coffee. I want to punch him. "Here, when they ring out the dead, two peals and three tolls means the dead person is a woman. Three peals and three tolls, a man."

205

A lump forms in my throat and I can't say a word. The hearse stops in front of the church. Two broad-shouldered men in suits get out. When one of them moves to open the back and pull out the coffin, I leap up and run into the bar to pay. I don't know what Pep is doing, I can't turn around.

I walk out, making sure not to look towards the church but I hear the metallic sound of what must be them unfolding the wheeled stand on which they will place that woman who's become a specific number of bell peals.

"Can we go?"

"Hey, what's the rush?"

He pulls on my arm to get me to sit down again. I have to turn my back on Pep to avoid seeing what's happening at the church door.

"I don't feel well. Let's go, please."

We don't speak on the way to the car. He puts an arm around my shoulder and pulls me closer to him. We walk like that for a good long while, but my body doesn't adapt to his, I feel my neck stiff, my mouth dry and I'm enveloped in a bad mood that's impossible to shake.

On the way back he looks at me obliquely as he drives and then places a hand on my thigh. Every time he touches me or kisses me when we aren't in the bubble of sex, something grates; I can't return his affection and I realize his attempts don't even make me feel affection for myself the way the same gestures between me and Mauro did. Of course, that was so long ago now, when things between Mauro and me were working, and affection was a natural part of that.

"If you want to rest, we can skip the hike we were planning."

"No, walking will do me good, really. I'm already feeling better, I'm really sorry. I got a little dizzy. It's nothing."

Another lie. I smile and take his hand.

We walk for almost two hours, first skirting various farmhouses and then climbing to a spring of freezing-cold water that flows from the rock face. The exertion and Pep, who's been telling war stories non-stop the whole way, have turned my mood around and I'm feeling like a person again. Lídia has sent me a short text insisting that I have fun; I deserve it, she says. And that she wants to hear all the details when I'm back. Three lines of emojis. I walk briskly up the mountain wondering if I have the right to hide behind a lie so I can feel like my old self again and enjoy a few fake days, but my reasoning is all jumbled, and I give up, tired of going round in circles.

Pep reaches the esplanade at the top long before I do and sits on a rock to wait for me. When I arrive he's staring out at the valley below, captivated. He doesn't realize I'm watching him and I relax, remembering Amsterdam. It was the snow, the intimacy of the snow, which worked to pause time briefly.

Later, when evening falls, in the white bathtub with golden feet bought in an antique shop and delivered to the little house in the lush forest, I'm sure I'm not the first little red riding hood who's bathed there. I allow myself the warm gift, these few exploratory days, that liquid silence marked only by a drop falling into the full tub, now one, then a few seconds later another, and on like that endlessly, marking a very slow rhythm but a rhythm nonetheless.

I put my big toe up against the tap to stop the improvised clock and its countdown. I think about what happened before in the town square, an uneasiness begins in my stomach and climbs up to my throat, desperate to find its way out. I know what it is, I know what it's about, and I have no choice but to make a decision.

It's nice inside the tub. The warm water mitigates the pleasant pain on the soles of my feet from the walking. As with a colour chart, when you know pain intimately you can make out a whole gamut of tones, and physical pain is never as dark as mental pain. I play at pushing my breasts out from under the bubbles and hiding them again, feeling my entire spine floating beneath the water, with no commitments or tasks to fulfil, without the responsibility of holding up a body and making it advance towards a resolution. I could remain like this and be a body without a soul, care for it with sex, give it pleasure, let it float in temperate water, swaddle it in the honesty of physical sensations, and distance it from any rational movement. So I ruminate and play with the water, ruminate and play until Pep comes in, with one dimple here and another there. He stares at me with that optimism of his, filled with wooden tables and delicious recipes.

"Did you know that these little white beans," he extends his palm to show me, "double in size when you soak them?"

And again that laughter shoots out of me, that laughter I thought had disappeared and, as I do every time it happens, I give Pep a kiss, poor Pep who doesn't know that it's a kiss of pure gratitude, and when he kisses me back, slightly suspicious, he tousles my wet hair and hands me a towel.

The hours advance, unstoppable and made of moments lived with the fragility of a dream: we speak in whispers, we look at each other intensely, and we laugh hard at things that may not be that funny, but we're trapped under the spell of novelty and physical attraction. I placed on the table the possibility of love, not love itself, and recalling that hypothesis becomes my centre of gravity.

"I have to go down to Barcelona this week to make a delivery; on Wednesday for sure, and maybe on Friday too. Do you want to do something on one of those days? Or both, if you feel like it. You think we could go to the cinema?" He widens his eyes excitedly with each question.

"I have to talk to my boss to see how these four days off play out," I lie. That was an easy one. "Maybe later, OK?"

"OK." He grabs his glass of wine without looking at me and takes a gulp. "So should I sign you up for the half-marathon on the first week of February that we talked about?"

"Whoa, Pep. I don't know if I'm in shape for that, honestly."

"You're quite fit, come on, don't be modest! It'll be fun."

"I'll let you know when I have my calendar in front of me, I have to check when my next few shifts are." I keep twisting the back of my earring. I take his face in my hands and smile.

I give him a very long kiss that leads to another, and yet another. I provoke him with my hands and tongue, set him aflame so he forgets all his questions. Amid the dance of arms, hands and legs, we reach his bedroom and make love with as much desire as ever, but I display more affection and devotion than the other times. I'm laying the groundwork and preparing my excuses.

When we caress each other he makes laboured noises, contented static, and I take the opportunity to confess in a whisper that I don't deserve him; he looks at me, wrinkling his brow, but he's too aroused to seek out some deeper meaning in what I've just said. He bites one of my breasts and it hurts, and then I stop making such an effort, I let myself go, and I study how to tell him what I've decided to tell him, but his pleasure is real and he deserves to believe that this last time will be as exceptional as all the others. I'm lying even with my body. But now, it's definite, and beneath my skin, the sensuality and play are already as obsolete as my visit here.

Later, carefree in the wake of his ecstasy, he tells me that in the summer he sleeps with the window open to hear the crickets, that he's ready for the good weather to begin.

"Just wait for the barbecues to start, out here with my friends."

The future is already here. The moment has come. I put a hand on his heart.

"Your heart is beating very slowly." I rest my face there so he can't see me.

"You killed me, you savage beast!"

210

I laugh but close my eyes in a nervous gesture.

"Thank you for taking care of me and feeding me, for the laughs, for the warmth of your home."

"Don't be silly. What are you saying?"

I lift my face to the height of his and I touch his hair.

"I'm going to leave first thing tomorrow morning."

"I know, doctor. A horde of miniature humans are expecting you."

I hold his gaze tenderly.

"And we won't see each other again, Pep."

He sits up, in two motions.

"Are you kidding me?"

"No. I'm sorry, Pep. I don't expect you to understand, but that's OK."

He gets angry and shouts at me. He uses swear words like "cunt" and "fucking hell" and says "fuck" over and over again. Why did I call him if all I wanted was to fuck? If I only wanted to fuck I could have told him I only wanted to fuck. I stoically bear the storm, I deserve it, and I feel comforted by his lack of pity for me.

We were just getting to know each other, he has no intention of tying me down or making plans for the future, but my call made him think I wasn't just looking for a roll in the hay. The expression *roll in the hay* sounds like it belongs to some distant period of my life, and I almost laugh. There is something about his tragic act that reeks of recycled lies.

"That's not what I wanted, Pep," I say very calmly, finally freed of having to come up with lies.

And he looks at me confused and I try to take his hand but he pulls it away. When he pauses I make sure he hears me when I say he is completely right, that I'm really sorry, and that it doesn't have anything to do with him.

Little by little he lowers his tone, just like a child's tantrum winding down when he knows there's no point and understands that no matter how much he cries he won't get what he wants. Finally, he puts on his pyjama bottoms and abruptly grabs the pillow and the blanket.

"It's two in the morning. There could be ice patches on the road. Sleep here, please."

He doesn't look me in the face. He slams the door and all the hostility and humiliation I've just thrown at him ricochet back onto me.

A few hours later neither of us has slept a wink. He comes back into the bedroom and gets into bed to spoon me from behind. He talks into my back and I feel the vibration of his voice inside the void of my body, returning the warmth.

"I'm sorry for speaking to you like that."

"It's OK, Pep."

"If you ever change your mind, you know where to find me."

I know that if I ever did look for him, he wouldn't be there, that he's got a rucksack filled with bullshit lines he can't hide, that if it's not me it'll be someone else, but that's not why I want to end it. I can only think about myself now. You can't build a house starting with the roof.

"Thank you, Pep. Really. For everything."

I leave when the day is beginning to lift. A thick fog insists on turning this goodbye into something sad. The car doesn't want to start. It's very cold and the frost has covered everything in a thin crust of white. It seems the sun won't come up today.

"Try it again."

Pep is leaning on the car door. I turn the key and after two attempts the engine finally turns over. We look at each other with resignation.

"We'll always have Amsterdam," he jokes, but his voice cracks a little, or maybe I just imagine that.

"Be well, Pep."

He closes the door and mouths the word goodbye, then leaves. He doesn't look back.

The lone woman again fills the inside of the car, with a volume and a weight I recognize instantly. I slowly retrace my route down the sandy road and when I come to the stop sign before the entrance to the winding road I feel a need to lower the window and breathe in the whole forest, so I can bring back home the sound of the river caressing the pebbles beneath the water, the scent of the rain that might fall, the freedom, the touch of Pep on my skin, the unmistakable pleasure of possibility, and the proof that I'm alive and have my whole life ahead of me. And then an owl alights from a twisted branch and quickly disappears among the holm oaks on the other side of the road. I can't see it anymore. I could have imagined it, dreamt it up perhaps, but something inside me comes undone, changes. The owl's flight lasted barely a few seconds. Just as long as magic lasts. Change is possible. Perhaps, after all, circling back to yourself is the best possible return.

* * * * * *

When I was little I wanted to become a nun like Maria von Trapp. I don't think I ever told you that. I wasn't drawn to life in the convent but I saw her passage through the church as necessary for all that came later. Soon I transformed my desire to be like her into the desire that someone like her would appear in my life, knocking on our door, suitcase in hand. Every night I would kneel by the bed, facing the window, and bring my hands together to pray that a Maria would show up in our lives. I was convinced my father needed a woman like her. I fantasized about Captain von Trapp and his daughter singing "Edelweiss" to the strumming of the guitar. I adapted that confirmation of Austrian patriotism into a love spell. The most obvious and necessary solution was to find someone for my father. There must have been women I never got to meet. Later, one day when I came home from secondary school, I crossed paths with one, her hair very dishevelled, in the hallway of our home. I never asked him about her and kept waiting for Maria, until one after the other all my myths came tumbling down.

As I fill up a glass vase with water and stand a eucalyptus branch in it, Lídia shares her opinion that at this point the most obvious and necessary solution is for me to find someone, to not be alone, I'm not saying you have to have

215

somebody move in with you, Paula, but you could use a little joy. I momentarily flee into the striking landscapes of the Austrian Alps and bite my tongue to keep from saying that there have been new men since you, men who were supposed to bring back joy and pleasure, and who did in some broken way, and if in the future there are more men (I also keep this to myself, although I know it's true) joy and pleasure will return mutilated like soldiers from this new war of mine.

I would give anything to know what's going through your mind, whether you think I'm exaggerating, to talk it over with you now that we wouldn't be a couple creating memories together anymore. I trust we'd have learnt to be good friends and that you'd sometimes come by the hospital to pick me up the way you used to, and I'd be able to explain to you that the obvious and necessary solution isn't finding someone else, not before reconfiguring myself as a person.

Then I would tell you all that stuff about *The Sound of Music* and you'd crack up laughing, and when we got home, I'd have invited you for supper, you'd turn up the thermostat because you're always cold and you would scratch your head as you searched for a botanical treatise on the shelves of the room that used to be your office, and you'd pull it out in that careful way you had with books, turning the pages until you found one that showed that flower which looks like white candyfloss and, raising your voice so I could hear you from the other room, you'd say yes, Paula, it's the flower from the Asteraceae family that grows in small clusters on high, rocky Alpine fields. *Leontopodium alpinum*, can you hear me?

And I would be sitting on the bed taking off my socks, and I'd smile to myself and release a contented sigh, and things between us would be at peace and as they should.

Lídia talks and talks and rearranges the eucalyptus branches and inside me there is only the echo of "Edelweiss", wrapped in that scent of endless winter.

* * * * * *

When I enter the building that houses Godó Media, on Diagonal near Francesc Macià, they make me show ID and then give me a visitor's pass. I leave behind the incessant roar of the Tuesday morning traffic and head down the hallway beneath the attentive gaze of a security guard who greets me with a lackadaisical nod. I soon realize that the attractive glass aesthetic of that modern building hides an entire world inside, just like the hospital where I work, except that here instead of medical staff and sick people there are mostly journalists. Journalists and sound technicians. Carla is a sound technician at a radio station. I never would have guessed that. Ever since I met her in the waiting room at the Hospital Clínic, I've been calling her the ballerina and imagining her gripping a barre and stretching her infinite legs out vertically, and then making flexible movements with her long, balanced body, spinning, her hair gathered up in a bun and her two small breasts, hard, like pure fibre. I've dreamt up festivals on a stage for her, with Mauro staring mouth agape, I've dressed her in a white tutu and covered her toes with blisters from the effort, with blood and sweat.

My stomach is queasy with the nervousness and shame of a little girl facing the monster under her bed. It's a cautious, calculated shame. We've communicated curtly through WhatsApp, without saying much, and both of us avoided emojis and exclamation marks. They would be unbefitting to the situation, as well as to the man we both loved, who now conclusively belongs to both of us. There's no longer any need for us to compete.

We agreed to meet on the fifth floor at eleven in the morning. She has a half-hour break between programmes but wrote "a quick half hour" and the adjective on the mobile screen made me imagine her naked, dropping white knickers with cartoon characters on them to the floor, skipping over to the shower and lathering up Mauro's rejuvenated body with soapsuds as they cackle with laughter.

I climb up the five flights, reminding myself that I was the one who suggested getting together and that it's too late to run away.

I see two men about my age laughing, talking about a third to whom they gifted a helicopter flight; from what they say, he was scared half to death. They're dressed casually, they seem carefree, and give off an image of boys or men who will never grow up, with perfectly sculpted beards, wearing cologne and trainers, and draped in an insouciance shared by the young woman at the reception desk and all the employees milling around on that floor.

"Good morning. I'm here to see Carla."

I realize I don't know her surname and I leave the sentence hanging in the air. It's not a problem, I'll soon learn that she's the only female sound technician on the staff. And

219

that she has a slight speech impediment that affects her "r"s, as well as a slight tic in her left eye, almost imperceptible but constant. Now I can imagine her better with Mauro, those slight imperfections I didn't notice at first glance must have gradually won him over, while I was immersed in dire patients and research articles.

"Hello, Paula."

She comes out to reception and greets me in a serious tone, a wary shadow in her gaze. She asks for five minutes and then sends me into the recording studio. She moves quickly, like everything in this place. I follow her with the awkwardness of someone entering unknown territory. Carla's index finger tells me to wait a second and I stand there like an idiot, my feet together and my hands in my jacket pockets. I want to leave. In a sudden frenzy a few days ago I thought it best to tidy everything up, prepare to close this chapter, get in touch with a ballerina who turned out not to be one and speak to her, but I'm not sure what I want to get out of it, and now the idea seems ridiculous. *You're already here, Paula, relax. You must be twice her age.* But it is her audacious youth that makes me swallow hard and close my eyes for a moment. I take a breath while she sits in front of a mixing table filled with channels and flickering lights. In front of her is a large window onto the studio with guests speaking live to a famous journalist whose name I can't remember. My nervousness puts incongruent ideas in my head, like taking his photo and sending it to my dad, but I refrain. *Don't be childish, Paula.* I wither more and more as the moments pass.

"Fifteen seconds, the piece ends, you come in and intro-duce the advert, OK? Relax, I'll edit it later."

Carla speaks quickly into an internal microphone to the journalist, stands and sits back down again, types, tidies some papers with a nervous energy that sets me on edge and then, without taking her eyes off the inside of the studio, gets up from the swivel chair and does a countdown on her fingers that transforms her into the most powerful woman I've seen: five, four, three, two, one. The world stops.

Everything in our lives was so predictable, I think, hyp-notized by her gesture: take out the rubbish when you leave, remember to buy water when you go past the supermarket, Sunday we can have lunch at my parents' house, I have a migraine, maybe tomorrow. I no longer wore perfume except when we went out for dinner with friends, and he refused to throw out those loafers I couldn't stand. It somehow seemed no man could resist this goddess in faded jeans and well-worn leather boots who counted down with her hands in the air. It wasn't feasible that you could resist a woman like that. It just wasn't an option.

She approaches me and suggests we leave through the same door through which we came in a moment ago. She takes me down the hall, skirting the recording studio, and I follow her like a frightened little dog. Hardly a trace remains of the confidence I had last night in front of the mirror, when I rehearsed a condescending speech, as if I somehow had the upper hand.

The views from up here are spectacular and the city, with

its constant chaos, looks easy to arrange tidily; I begin to sense that everything would be simpler if I could manage to look at it from another perspective but, for the moment, every thought keeps leading me back to the same bewildered state.

We sit in a small room far from the din. There are only two armchairs, a round table with all of today's newspapers and a machine with tea and coffee. She offers me a drink and makes two coffees before sitting down.

I look at her arse while her back is turned. Her jeans hug her butt with an almost unfair generosity, as if they'd been tailor-made to a standard of beauty we all helplessly admire. Despite her svelteness, there is a sensuality to her curves that makes her desirable. I think how lucky Mauro must have felt.

She sits down. She crosses her legs and sighs.

"How are you?" she asks in a wounded voice.

How is it possible I didn't speak first? I'm paralysed.

"Getting by. And you?"

She lowers her gaze and focuses on her coffee. She slowly stirs the little plastic spoon and inhales noisily before speaking, her body widening as if an umbrella were opening in her ribs.

"Not so hot."

Her response reminds me why I'm here and suddenly Mauro makes his presence known. Unconsciously I inch towards her like a mother concerned about her daughter's delicate situation, and I put a hand on her thigh until her look makes it clear that she doesn't appreciate it. I pull away brusquely.

"What did you want to talk about?"

For the first time I notice the tic in her eye. She contracts the lid involuntarily. It occurs to me that perhaps she hasn't always had it, maybe it was brought on by the trauma of Mauro's death. I quickly review the possible neurological disorders of the central nervous system. *She isn't a patient, for the love of God, Paula. Focus!* I banish the thought but realize I'm lost.

"What did you say?" I ask nervously.

"Why did you want to meet up? Is there something you need?"

I think carefully before speaking. Yes. There is something I need. And I say it.

"I need to know when it all started."

She sighs loudly and takes a sip of coffee.

"It all started here." She nods, indicating the radio station in general. "Mauro and his partner Nacho came with a writer they were promoting."

"That Russian woman?"

She nods. I remember the Russian woman and the days around her promotional visit. Mauro was so busy I hardly saw him, and incredibly excited.

"I had read her book and really enjoyed it. Normally it's not something I do, but I wanted to chat to her and ask her to sign my copy…" She pauses, gathers her hair behind her head with one hand and places it to one side of her shoulder. "I speak Russian."

She speaks Russian. Of course. That must have clinched it. Mauro must have melted instantly, despite her speech impediment.

I unfold calendar pages in my mind, trying to remember when that all happened, when he came home with the Russian woman's novel hot off the press, happy as a kid with new shoes, and I start to feel panicky. It's been almost a year since the accident and the past has already become unrecognizable. I stopped using a system of time divided up into months, weeks and days. Now it's been reduced to the simple duality of before and after, and I shield myself behind my coral reef. Everything that happened before seems as remote as if it had happened to someone else. Time has blurred it all like a wet blot on a watercolour.

She realizes I'm blocked but does nothing.

"Did he tell you from the beginning that he was in a relationship?" I manage to articulate the question.

"I figured it out because he didn't ask me anything about my personal life."

His typical avoidance, I think, and smile sarcastically.

"I never asked him to leave you, but his mind was so set…"

Her gaze drifts out over endless Barcelona, past the Diagonal, and I want to shake her, make her spit out all the details.

"What do you mean?" I say with feigned calmness.

"Just that, that he quickly decided to move forward with the wedding, and that was when he told me that he had to tell you first, leave home and make sure that you were OK."

My stomach churns. It stings as if I'd been punched. I'd guessed something from the conversations on his mobile, but they hadn't gone that far. The word *wedding* hits my forehead, right between the eyes, and gives way to a headache that I know will become intense pain and nausea if I don't take a pill quickly. I look at her hands in fear and see no ring.

"Did you get married?" I ask in a reedy voice.

"No. We didn't have time." She gets choked up. She brings her hands to her face.

"I'm sorry," I mutter, but it's not true, I'm not sorry at all.

"We already had a date set at Santa Maria del Mar." She pauses to take a breath. She keeps her gaze on the horizon. A church wedding. He wanted to get married and maybe have the child I never gave him. Her eyes are flooded and a tear slips, almost like an invertebrate being, down her face. Her cheeks are pink from the heating, the same cheeks that Mauro must have covered in clandestine kisses that would later become public, permitted, innocuous. Those domestic pressures that had hemmed me in for years were now materialized in a young, pretty, sad woman. Here you have it, Paula. How old is she? Twenty-six, twenty-seven? Thirty at most? Her gaze is clear, her reproductive potential at its height.

"How old are you?"

"Excuse me?" she asks, somewhere between offended and stunned. She spins a little golden ball that hangs from a thin gold chain around her neck.

"How old are you? You're obviously much younger than I am," I blurt out.

"Twenty-nine." And she stares at me, defiantly.

You hit the nail on the head, Paula. He needed someone with a high ovarian reserve.

225

"He talked about you often. He told me a lot about your work."

He didn't talk about me, I think. He talked about my work.

"Oh, really?" I am trying to be nice but having trouble connecting. I'm still at the wedding.

"I brought you some things I found around the house. I think you should have them and besides… it hurts me to look at them. It irritates me to have them around. I'll give them to you when we leave."

"What things?" I ask, and I think about the hurt and irritation, about the dimensions of her irritation, how she is a new irritation for me but I've been one for her for longer.

"The bag he used to bring over to spend the night." She aims and throws the paper coffee cup into a bin and starts to speak more dynamically. "I don't know, some clothes, a toothbrush, a manuscript, oh, yeah, and a bag of dried leaves," she says, downplaying the treasure she's been bequeathed.

"A what?" I ask.

"For tea. You know him." And the present tense makes my heart skip a beat.

We both smile. For a moment, the leaves knit a passing connection. Mauro grew aromatic plants to make infusions. He would put them in transparent bags with labels: lemon balm, mint, thyme, camomile. I can almost hear him. "Help me move this pot, Paula. Thyme likes partial shade and it's getting too much sun here. Let's bring it over to that corner." And me, stopping him, laughing. "Mauro, the neighbours are going to report us—this is starting to look like the Amazon jungle… God knows what animals could come out from that thicket!" Amused, he would scratch his nose with the back of his sand-covered hand and say, "Come on, shut up and pull it this way." I'm flooded with emotion but I keep it under control.

I think about the percentage of life the two of them shared, what was left on his mobile, and I add in everything the phone didn't save. The resulting figure is proportional to all the pain that landed on me like an unexpected slap. I don't understand how those dried leaves could irritate her. She must be stupid not to want to hold on to them.

"If you think about it," she adds distractedly with a slight shrug, "his family doesn't even know me. I wanted to take things more slowly and he always said that there was no need to wait for Santa Maria del Mar, that we could get married on our own, without telling anyone."

And I thought about the money they wanted me to inherit, the bedspread, the Bohemian crystal, and I realize that Mauro wouldn't have had the courage to face up to his mother, to her despotic authority. Mauro had that cowardly side to him, of course he hadn't brought Carla into his family orbit and told them that I was out. After all, with Carla he was still in the throes of the wide-eyed love of every new relationship. Sweet and powerful. If he had died later, with the bells of Santa Maria del Mar still echoing in his head, she would now be wearing a ring on her finger, and she would be the widow.

On the way out we pass the studio with the guests laughing and speaking blithely. Watching them, it seems that the two of us are coming from a distant place where we've spent a long time, all the time needed to take other people's laughter and joy as an insult, all the time needed to understand that there is something sad and vaguely contemptible when love fades, but it's nothing like the annihilating defeat of death. We believe we've got it domesticated with rituals, mourning, symbols, colours, but it remains wild and free. Death is always the one in charge. Death controls life and never the other way around.

Carla hands me Mauro's bag, which is super heavy because of the manuscript.

"Oof, it's like a body bag!"

I'm surprised by my flippancy. It frightens me to realize that, somehow, a chapter has ended.

We say goodbye with a sterile peck on each cheek. Even her crisp scent is perfect, yet she was obviously willing to risk it all to be with Mauro. Before I turn and leave, I thank her for meeting up with me. She puts her hands in the pockets of her jeans and lengthens her body, growing a little taller. She bestows on me a bitter smile that I imagine is her way of saying "you're welcome". That vein of hostility between us is keeping Mauro alive, and we'll continue to work together, as rivals, to that end.

"Infant respiratory distress. Pili, we have to administer sur-
factant. Please check the mother's chart. I need to know if
she's been given glucocorticoids."

Outside it's been raining for a while. Full black night.
The water is a murmuring interrupted only by the rhythm
of the machines in the room. I examine the babies born
while I was away for a few days. Two of them are new,
one will be fine, no repercussions, if we can get his lungs
to mature. I'm convinced we will, there's a hint of strength
in every spasm of his little hands. The other is a little girl
born at twenty-seven weeks whose mother has put her up
for adoption. She has necrotizing enterocolitis and they've
had to operate. She isn't improving, she's in shock and
bleeding frequently. The accursed phrase no one wants
to have to declare is on the whole team's lips: "Nothing
can be done." The tiny girl isn't responding. Her situation
is irreversible. It's only a matter of time. I avoid looking
into her miniature face when I examine her. I don't dare
to meet her blind eyes and let her know that she has no
one else, no one who will say goodbye to her. Pili's deep
sigh is the starting shot for the release of an impotence
that's been engraved into our tone of voice and the soles
of our clogs for hours, into the weight of our steps, slower

around the incubator where she awaits the inevitable with alarming dignity.

"What time are you having supper? I'm leaving now." In Spanish, of course.

"No, I'm not hungry." In Catalan. "I want to stay with her. You go on. I'll have a coffee later."

"Do you want me to stay?"

My imploring gaze says yes and she gets it right away. Intuition is a nurse dressed in white who rolls up her sleeves and washes her hands and arms up to the elbows while she deciphers the tension in my jaw.

There is no need to say a word. We open the incubator. Pili holds her by her tiny head. Before I touch her, I rub my hands together hard so they won't be so cold; if only I could rub my heart like that, my stomach, if only I could rub my soul like that. I hold up the baby's feet, I run my index finger over her palms, which are two small stars silhouetted against the sky blue of the clinical nest, I trace every recess of her damp skin that isn't covered in tubes. I think about the osteopath, about the day he made me laugh when he said that if he ever had children he'd name them after all the corpuscles in the skin. Meissner, Pacini, Ruffini and Krause. Eric and his touch, how he increased oxytocin levels and dressed up his study with terminology that spoke of sensory innervation, about the role of touch within a somatosensory system, and as he explained it I understood it more simply: that sharing the intimacy of skin, holding hands, transmitting physical affection could make a difference to a premature newborn, just as it could to a gaunt woman in her early forties.

It won't be long before we take her off life support and leave her with just analgesics, but we stroke her for a little longer there inside, with hands and arms cradled in the warmth of her heated crib.

"I'm going to hold her," Pili says. I look at her and nod. I'm the one who should take that decision, but we are alone, the diagnosis is done and approved, and it's Pili who has access to a sixth sense without the conscious intervention of reason. We are overcome by a wave of satisfaction for the mute decision we have just taken: we will accompany that lone being who is fading with each heartbeat and we will be part of the small world who knew her over the last three days. We will be there, we will form part of the dust of life that she will have been. We won't leave her alone. Pili and I will take turns, along with the other consultant. We will hold her in our arms, switching turns every half hour.

As dawn approaches I realize there are tears falling on the little girl. My tears. I'm surprised. We move in silence. The consultant brings me some gauze to use as a handkerchief and asks me if I want water, or anything else. I've decided that I want the impossible, to save her and resuscitate Mauro so I can explain to him how unfair things are sometimes, and have everything start over. I just whisper no, thanks, and shake my head.

The whole unit exudes a strange atmosphere. The ceiling lights fill the rooms with additional heat and an artificial peace. Everything seems on alert, even the sweet, innocent newborns. Something hovers ominously and we await it with our heads bowed.

Everything and everyone does their part, cogs in the hospital machine: the clock hands advance indifferently; the nurses dart wherever they are called; the doctors make decisions, some more resolute than others; the cleaning ladies flash tired smiles, bags under their eyes; the parents watch the future hopefully through the incubators; the young man sits on a sofa for the last hour and a half with a baby on his chest, skin to skin; the incessant rain; Mahavir is finally sleeping fitfully in the HDU; life advances second by second, and death corners it in the hallways and lifts, no traps necessary.

There is an uptick of tension when we pull out her IV and a respectful, tragic silence when Pili hands me the little one. Mine will be the last arms that cradle her. And then death snatches her from me without thinking twice, carries her off, but I got there in time and feel I've won the match. I'm here. I'm by her side.

All of us there in the room hug each other. Sighs, a few curses. The monitors and their respective alarms mark a beat that reminds us that life goes on. Beep-beep, the constant sound of the calm of the ICU. The full delivery rooms, the traffic and the winter, the bad news, the good, the news of no significance at all, the metro underground and an aeroplane up in the sky, the keys like words beneath my father's fingers, the man praying at the chapel with all his hopes pinned on a Christ made in a carpentry workshop, the buzzing of espresso machines, the photo of Mum and her smile in black and white. The blinds that rise, the burners on the stove, the stream of cold water in the shower and someone singing oblivious to it all, the sea, the forest. Cash machines spitting out notes, nervous mice inside cages, clouds pushed by the wind, and the shapes we give them, an old woman at a spinning wheel, a man walking a French bulldog, a starter dough activating the microbes in another starter dough, and cargo ships coming into port and heading out again. And the plants. The plants growing and extending their roots below ground in a parallel world.

We disband and each decamp to our own spots, busy again, like insects working: checking, monitoring, supervising, thinking, forgetting. I run to the shift room. I flee, I should say. I don't know how long I've been there but no one came looking for me until just a few minutes ago, when Pili entered the darkness.

"Paula?"

She doesn't turn on the light but she draws back the opaque curtain and day enters coquettishly. I know she's seen my face but she doesn't say anything. She sits down beside me, on the floor, slowly lowering herself with a slight groan.

"Why don't you come over to my house today? My daughters will be there for lunch and Sandra's bringing the baby. The two of them have been driving me crazy over the wedding dresses. That way you can meet them."

We both sit down with our backs against the wall. I draw my knees to my chest and Pili has her thick legs stretched out on the cold tiles. The edges of white cotton socks stick out from the tops of her clogs, a slice of her legs showing below the trousers of her scrubs. They remind me of the cotton socks my mother used to buy me for Easter, which I would wear with my new shoes in spring and early summer. Later I was the one who had to remind Dad that the heat was coming and I needed new shoes and cotton socks. It's possible that in his world of melodies and birds, little girls went barefoot. Our memories select events that were neutral at the time; and as they happened, as we pulled on new cotton socks, we couldn't be aware of creating a unique memory of a mother we would soon lose. Socks can be extraordinary. Socks, on the day that everything falls apart, can be a mother.

It's the first time I've ever seen Pili sitting on the floor in all these years. It's as if her hospital disguise has fallen away leaving only the woman who, despite having worked all night long, already has lunch prepared for her daughters and grandson, the woman who always smells of tropical fruit shampoo and fabric softener. I hear her breathing beside me. We are exhausted. The first time I cried over a patient's death was during my first year as a resident. Santi told me to pull myself together and not take it personally, otherwise I would never become a good neonatologist.

"When a child is born in a critical condition, fighting for their life is as important as not fighting. It's as important to know how to save them as it is to know how to let them die." And I pulled myself together.

—

I know that in my tears today hides a little girl sitting in class with the animal kingdom explained on the blackboard, a girl upon whom a crushing weight has fallen again, a weight that's incalculable to those who've never lost anyone, those still safe on the other side. A titanic weight of resentment and rage and so much pain, a weight that finally goes through the earth and down into the depths, sending up vertical walls topped with spikes, and from its darkness emerge crows that fly over the entrance and ensure no one can come in. That is yours and only yours. Here. Cry, for once and for all. Rend your heart, if you want, no one will understand you because here inside there is nothing to understand. Grab hold of it. It's yours and only yours and you will never feel a stronger weight of ownership. It's untransferable. Don't try to share it, you'll turn it into a joke. It is the void, the absence, all the longing turned into a bottomless hole. Although all of us on this side have one, none resembles another, every witness must bear their own and survive a unique version. A new place. Welcome. On the other side they don't call it a void and they can't see the crows. On the other side they search for aphorisms like the ones I used to search for to illuminate the faces of desperate parents. I would tell them that time heals, that they had to be strong and look to the future. What did I know about the void? Not a damn thing. I couldn't foresee the crows guarding the entrance unique to each father, to each mother, to each shattered heart. Cry, Paula. You couldn't save him. Understand now how important it is to let him die.

Pili doesn't touch me, she doesn't hug me, her hands are in the pockets of her lab coat. She doesn't look at me either, she talks as she lets her eyes fall onto first one wall, now the next, as if distracted and not wanting to let the strain show in her voice. She knows me well, she knows how much physical proximity I can tolerate.

"I made some sauce the other day and we can pick up some fresh fish on the way. You stop in front of the market, wait with your hazards on and I'll run in. It'll be empty now."

I don't answer. I wipe the water and snot streaming from my nose with the cuff of my sweater pulled over my fist. I try to imagine the scene in all its ordinariness. The car, the calm. A market. I like that everyday moment, that pause in the battle we just fought. I look at her. I would like to tell her that the last time I went to the market, when I'd spent ten minutes in the queue for the fishmonger's, I turned around and left, unable to listen to more conversations about family meals. I wanted to buy a hake fillet. A small portion—individual and ridiculous—of hake, and I had to put up with whole families, bones that had to be removed for angelic children, caramelized couples with no apparent cracks and sunny weekends featuring the first person plural. The "we" consumes fish, the "we" gathers people around a table, the "we" grows strong and makes a team. But I don't tell her that because I don't have the energy to explain the nuances.

"Look, since you aren't going to say anything, I'll say it. Come over for lunch, Paula, it's decided. Now get up, wash your face and blow your nose, honey, you're a disgusting mess. Come on, I need ten minutes to change. We'll take your car. I'll meet you in the garage."

She gets up with the same rusty rhythm she'd had lowering herself down into my well a few minutes ago and I take her warm plump hand as if I don't want to let her go. I knew how her hand would feel, feminine, protective, identical to the memory of my mother. Skin-to-skin contact during the neonatal period affects adult behavioural expression. Without the comfort of touch, full physical and emotional development isn't possible. We need to be caressed when we aren't yet someone in order to know how to relate when we become people of whom so much is expected. I touch Pili's hand as if it was the last life raft on a sinking ship.

"We'll get some dessert. We deserve it."

"That's my Paula."

A possessive, and you become somebody.

At the table I feel reborn, so distracted I forget myself. Sandra and Lara, Pili's daughters, greet me with hugs and joyful expressions. It's like we've known you all our lives, Mum talks about you so much! The shadow hastens to mutter that she must have told them about my catastrophe, but soon a baby comes crawling in with a sleepy face and grabs all the attention. He's the son of Sandra, Pili's youngest, who is getting married in two weeks to his father, although they'd separated before the boy was born. While Pili loads the plates she serves up a life lesson. I learn what love in all caps is. It has to do with the murmur of voices, with the precise amount of food that Pili knows each person wants on their plate, with how they pass the bread basket, it has to do with the bread basket itself, lined in white cloth tipped with lace, with the nervous expectation and exhaustion for an impending wedding, lists, guests who called, aunties who told Pili she can come over to pick up the corsage ornaments they made by hand. It has to do with the hope a mother puts in her daughters, with the intimacy of an argument between sisters over leaving the keys at the salon so she doesn't have to come by just to get them, with how Mum breaks it up with a "That's enough. You're too old for this. Leave the keys with me and your father will bring them, see how easy it is?"; and the revealing words echo inside me, see how easy it is, Paula, see how easy true love is.

We say goodbye amidst well wishes, flattery and general pandemonium and I head out onto the street leaving behind their ordinary lives, devoid of real adversity. I don't know where I am, I don't know the neighbourhood and I have trouble finding the car park where we left my car. The din of a bus, store windows announcing sales, puddles of rain reflecting the opening sky, a scrawny dog with bulging eyes that barks as I rush by, banners advertising a music festival and, finally, the "P" signalling the car park. I stop short to hold in the familiarity of Pili's home and I'm overcome by the pressing need to make a call.

"Hi, Dad. It's me."

[...]

"No, everything's fine, don't worry. But, are you busy this evening?"

* * * * * *

Today is my birthday.

I'm forty-three.

The age you were.

Thinking that is the strangest thing I've ever experienced.

When I blew out the candles on the cake it was as if I'd gone deaf, my ears clogged. If they'd used forty-three individual candles maybe I would have taken away a different impression, Mauro, but Lídia bought a red four and three, big as day, impossible to downplay, and my legs turned to mush. You will always be forty-three and I get a cold shiver when I think that.

There was a lot of background noise, you know how they are. Imagine a surprise party hosted by Lídia. Even Vanesa and Marta came. In just two weeks their rotation will be over and I'm already missing them. They've become the life of the department, splattering me with their folly and their contagious laughter, pushing me through this harsh year. I'll always appreciate that.

I still have a headache. The flat is a mess. The floor is covered in confetti and sticky trails. I'm sorry to tell you that, you would have got very nervous seeing all those glasses of wine and cava spilling on the sofa. Luckily it's not your sofa anymore. Besides, you don't know it but, since you've been gone, the gang has been popping out babies like rabbits and they bring them everywhere, which I can't understand. All I'll say is that kids like chocolate. But that's how it should be, Mauro. It's time to get this house dirty, fill it with noise, find the bathroom occupied and later the toilet clogged with a roll of paper. To steal affection from wherever it can be found. From friends, neighbours, the smile of the car park attendant. To blow out candles and be able to wish for something that isn't the impossible: bringing you back.

This time no one gave me presents of books or plants, but a ton of clothes that tasted of springtime and a straw hat too. I put it on, so embarrassed, and Nacho said I was radiant, that lately I'd been glowing. I knew he was exaggerating but I let him do it and gave him a kiss on the cheek. Which is a little like giving one to you. There's a lot of you in him and a lot of me in you.

I was waiting for the doorbell to ring and for you to appear behind the green leaves of something potted. Wave you in and say to everyone, look who's here! Later I stopped waiting for you and gave in to the effort they were all making to celebrate my birthday. I found Martina, Lídia's youngest, standing stock still in our bedroom. She looked at me with that suspicious, wise face of hers, with her hair in bunches and a parting down the middle.

"Where's Mauro?"

We observed each other carefully, the way people who share grave knowledge tend to do. In the background, laughter and the hum of life. With a nod I pointed to the photo of Midsummer Eve on top of the table beside what is now my bed. She looked back over at me with an amused expression and left skipping down the hall. We've explained to her, several times, that you've died, but every once in a while she asks for you. The years will pass and I'll grow old, shrink a centimetre or two, my hair will turn white, I'll have wrinkles all over, and you and I will always be there in that photo, me in the past and you in the present. I'm with Martina on this one, there is something uncertain that leaves room for doubt, that confers the right to only half-believe the truth, that prefers to keep asking where you are every day, like a secret only some of us can comprehend.

Today I turned forty-three. I caught up with you and I still don't understand how that could have happened.

* * * * * *

AFTER

Thomas took off his shoes on the terrace. I don't get why he does that. He walks around barefoot all day, his soles black and his heels cracked. I didn't say anything though. This is going to be his home now, he can walk around however he likes. It's April and he's already wearing Bermuda shorts like a reminder of the tourist he once was. We've been working for hours. We came from the garden shop so loaded down it took us three trips from the car to get all the plants, flowers, pots, topsoil, rose soil mix and ericaceous compost for the camellias and azaleas. We'd asked for everything with the nervousness of someone setting off on a definitive voyage, overcome with the excitement of what we were about to do. We'd been consulting one of Mauro's notebooks where I'd discovered the sketch of his initial design for the terrace. We followed the explanations of the salesperson helping us with our epic task. Next to the drawing was a basic list with everything he'd planned for making his garden. A list that Mauro kept adding to until it became his biography.

I left the car with Thomas and he picked me up at the hospital around noon because the garden centre that he'd promised me had everything was on the way. Of course he was late and of course we got lost somewhere between Barcelona and Castelldefels. I didn't get cross, actually I couldn't help but laugh when we passed the Riviera for the third time. It's easy to laugh on a dual carriageway, with a good friend, and especially with the memory of that morning fresh in my mind. At 11.44 a.m. I signed Mahavir's discharge from the hospital.

I lifted my head and saw a burst of colour when Mahavir's parents entered. His mother wore a colourful embroidered sari to celebrate bringing her son home, and in her arms was Mahavir, wrapped in colourful linen, those little black eyes I'd studied for months now smiling. The emotion and gratitude from his family inspired the entire team. His mother gave us jasmine flowers and all the women put them in their hair. She also brought us some *vada* she'd made that night, a savoury snack I gobbled down with the satisfaction of celebrating life. Mahavir means "hero". His father told me that ages ago, when the tiny being who fit into one hand was fighting for this discharge today. From now on, my advice for everyone expecting a child will be to find an appropriate name, think long and hard about the meaning they wish to give to the person they're carrying inside. After our celebration, I watched my hero head off, asleep in the pram his father was pushing out into the world beyond, while his mother, petite and filled with light, turned and, with her palms pressed tightly together, whispered for the last time:

"Namaste, Dr Cid."

"Namaste," I replied.

Suddenly the past flooded in.

—

It was that Wednesday in February when I first got word of Mahavir. He was a foetus inside his mother and every member of the obstetrics and neonatology team was already studying him in full detail in order to determine whether she should be admitted early because of high risk. I was paying attention to the meeting, but checking my watch often; I had a lunch date with Mauro and was all aflutter. I had put on the earrings he liked. I'd made a decision the night before and wanted to announce it at lunch, I didn't think I'd be able to wait until the dessert course. A desire to reproduce, my first and only to date, had bloomed suddenly in the biscuit aisle of the supermarket the Saturday before. Mauro was looking for something with organic seeds and there was a boy of three or four next to him, pointing up at a package on the top shelf. He tousled his hair and picked the boy up so he could reach the biscuits. And that was enough. That single gesture. I didn't say anything. When I tried to reflect on it everything fizzled out, if I tried to write it, it was even worse, so I tiptoed around the thought that refused to leave me and, that night when Mauro was out, I decided that the very next day I would tell him that maybe it was too late, that it would be risky and I wasn't a hundred per cent convinced, but that yes, since he'd been so sure all those years and as long as I didn't have to give up my career, we could try to have a baby. I wanted to tell him that it was a crazy idea, that I felt almost feverish and slightly delirious, but that we should just run with it, that I couldn't think of a better way to solve what was going on with us, what we couldn't name.

I wanted to tell him that I was determined to fix whatever it was, that I wanted to make things good between us. I had memorized a short speech. A child should be a whim, Mauro, a wish made on a birthday cake. The time had come. I exited a car park by the beach. I was walking with my back very straight and my head held high and with each step I repeated: wish, whim, wish, whim, wish, whim. I stopped at a red light and started up again. Wish, whim, wish, whim. Mauro was already waiting for me at the restaurant. He'd come on his bicycle. He seemed to have something up his sleeve. My words fled my mind with his first thin smile. My mood soured and I deflated. I couldn't tell him all that when he had such a nasty expression on his face. I thought maybe later that day, and then the sonogram of Mahavir we'd been studying at the hospital a few hours earlier came into my head. Was it ethical to bring that child into the world? Was it ethical to bring others into the world when wishes and whims can sour so abruptly? The sea swept away my titanic thought with its coming and going beyond the windows and I felt Mauro far away from me, talking about trivial things, a book he'd read, a distributor he'd been to see, that the Renfe was a disaster and his train had arrived half an hour late. He had a concrete weight to his voice, spoke in short sentences, as if he were tossing out bread crumbs to find his way back if he got lost after dropping his bomb. And, without waiting for the sweetness of dessert, he dropped it. Bombs are bombs, indiscriminate projectiles unable to land with precision. The impact took out everything around it. Even his own life.

A few months later, with the wounds still open and my heart torn, they placed Mahavir in my hands in the delivery room, handing over the human side of the war. I calculated the weight of a hero, I intubated him and handled him with the urgency of keeping him alive and the clairvoyance to understand that my whim and my wish would always be focused on having control over the fate of these babies who would never be mine.

Leaving requires a liturgy that helps transform endings into new beginnings. Mahavir did it this morning, and now it's time for me to do it as well.

When we had everything ready to start working on the terrace, I was struck by the image of Thomas, his back to me, hands on his waist, not knowing where to start. He was smoking a cigarette in front of the chaos of the dark, damp, turned-over earth, and seeing him I felt lost. I had the sensation we were about to profane a tomb. But then he spoke and I clung to his calm.

"We'll pull out the bamboo. It's an invasive species."

I slapped him lightly on the thigh with a glove.

"You're the invasive species. The bamboo stays."

He laughed and took a sip of beer while I sought shelter in the joke. I don't know what it was, but I noticed it then. I succumbed to a feeling like the end of holidays, when summer towns empty of the everyday life that's filled them for weeks. Big changes have that, you perceive them in small signs. Then the feeling scattered like pollen. We continued on the terrace for quite a while, fertilizing the earth, placing the plants near where they would go and, just like that, I started ripping out all of Mauro's dead plants and, when I had finished, worn out, a strange cry came out of me, filled with triumph and agony. I shake the dirt off my arms and run a hand over my brow. I feel very strong, I could take on giants.

We take a break. If we don't finish today we'll finish this weekend. My neck is stiff and my arms hurt. There are still things to do in the flat, like clean, put everything in boxes, change the electricity, gas and water bills out of my name and into Thomas's. Negotiate with the movers, set up direct debits for everything again, speak to the owner, collect my Jurassic answering machine with Dad's voice inside it. There are things to do like get dressed, eat and take a last look around the bedroom, now completely emptied of everything and of us. All that's left is that aged parquet flooring we trod on best we knew how. The parquet and the old iron radiator painted white, where we would glue our butts on winter evenings as we told each other about our days, Mauro would meticulously trim his fingernails and I would remove my mascara with a cotton ball. We were all those moments. We filled that house with small sounds that now echo in the emptiness, sounds that ended up demarcating our dialogue. Memories are malleable and it's easy to correct them, you can trim them and place them on a different background, succumb to our modern vices and retouch them, play with filters that embellish, and patch together a past to challenge the flesh-and-blood present in which there's no need to be so intransigent because, in our solitude, there's no one to point out that that shadow wasn't there, or that that corner was better lit.

Thomas has been gradually adapting to the rhythm of the space. His tranquility doesn't seem affected by my anxious calls, to the movers who are running late, and to my father, who has insisted I sleep at his place until I'm settled into my new flat. Thomas brought down his record player, which already occupies a special place in the dining room. He keeps appearing in the doorway with a handful of records and slowly placing them on the exact same shelf just one floor down; his main priority is alphabetical order, he doesn't care when I remind him that the smoke extractor needs fixing and to turn it on he'll have to first press the second button from the left.

"Counting Crows, Bob Dylan, Ben Harper, Fleetwood Mac." He makes a list in his strong, rough New York accent that lends him a touch of exotic urbanity.

"And don't forget: on Wednesday they're coming about the boiler!" I shout from the terrace.

"Oscar Peterson, Tom Petty, Lou Reed, Stevie Wonder. You have to hear this song, Paula!"

I don't know what's playing, a woman's deep, subdued voice, recorded live. The volume is turned way up and the audience's cheering fills every room. I kneel down to touch the tender leaves of a new plant.

"You'll have a laugh with this guy, I'm sure of that," I say to it in a whisper. Then I stand up with a lump in my throat. I glance around to address all the plants we've just bought.

"You'll be happy here. Living is worth the effort. It's hard sometimes, I won't lie, but I promise you it's worth it."

"It was recorded in '76!" he says in Spanish, then switches to English to add, "Isn't it amazing?"

His tinny voice reverberates through the empty spaces, and I envy his unassuming happiness, his musical idyll. The effortlessness of it makes me smile.

Our house had been waiting for you, Mauro. The doors and the windows observed me attentively, they stealthily studied my movements, perhaps convinced that your return depended on me. If I opened the kitchen cabinets, the quantity of cups and cutlery and wine glasses questioned me, asking for you with an impudence that was hard to bear, like your terrace's descent to hell, as it wept and longed for you, because there are no shortcuts around the pain of a loved one's death. There really aren't, despite the small victories: we can forgive each other unilaterally, grasp our fragility, accept that the memories are the closest thing to having you near; I can learn to play the piano, even let my father teach me, buy an old motorcycle and park it on a new corner in a neighbourhood that's more my style, live in a flat with a balcony, and finally throw away your mobile phone and with it everything that doesn't belong to me. I need to stay on my toes, keep pulling tiny newborns towards the light, who knows, maybe even fall in love again someday. But I definitely need to start fresh, and admit that death, just sometimes, is an opportunity. I'm not running away, Mauro. I'm just leaving. I'll come back every once in a while to say hi to the plants and I won't forget about your death. Forgetting it would be letting you die a second time and that—you can rest assured—won't happen.

Thomas comes out onto the terrace with a handful of strawberries. He approaches and offers me one. I refuse with a wave of my hand. He chews slowly and looks around abstractedly. Spring embraces everything. A blackbird whistles from a nearby rooftop. The sun is about to set and now is when birdsong is most intense.

"*Turdus merula*," I murmur.

"What's that?" he asks in Spanish.

"A blackbird. Hear it?" I answer in Catalan. *Una merla. La sents?*

"I don't know what a *merla* is." He shrugs, indifferent. "Wait a sec, you've got an eyelash."

He delicately lifts it off my cheekbone and I note a rising blush when his face is close to my hair. The last rays of sun gild his features. He takes me by the wrist and opens my hand. He places the eyelash in the middle of my palm like a watchmaker moving the tiny pieces of the works in a timepiece that's opened up wide.

"Throw it over your shoulder." In English.

"No, here we blow them, Thomas." In Catalan.

Smiling, tickled like children, we spend a moment discussing the trajectory the eyelash should take. The new plants, who don't know us, observe us from their soil and adapt to the joy floating in the atmosphere. They take it as a cue, as they should.

"C'mon! Make a wish!"

My heart leaps, and blowing an eyelash feels like the oracle that will decide my fate. I squeeze my eyes shut as tightly as I can, they burn inside and my lids are as wrinkled as parchment. In the dark, a dance of phosphenes begins, stimulated by the retina that creates the illusion of light and motion, and I think of ghosts but hasten to remember that this terrace will be a vestige of your life, Mauro, not a stone monument to your death. And then I do it, I take in air as if my life depended on it and I make a wish for myself, wishing as hard as I can.

ACKNOWLEDGEMENTS

Very special thanks to Dr Maria Camprubi of the Rheumatology Unit at the Hospital Sant Joan de Déu in Barcelona, for sharing her time and expertise.

ACKNOWLEDGEMENTS

Very special thanks to Dr Marta Camprubí, of the Neonatology Unit at the Hospital Sant Joan de Déu in Barcelona, for sharing with me her knowledge and experience of the important work she does.

Thanks to Adam Freudenheim and the whole team at Pushkin Press for believing in this story and bringing it to English-language readers.

Thanks to my agent, Bernat Fiol of SalmaiaLit, for his professionalism and conviction.

Thanks to Mara Faye Lethem, for putting such care into the translation and creating an identical twin for my Paula in English.

Thanks to Art Omi for allowing Mara and me the opportunity to work together, side by side, at their Translation Lab residency to polish this English version.

And thanks to my sons Ignasi and Oriol, for making the sun come up every day.

THE PASSENGER

ULRICH ALEXANDER BOSCHWITZ

LEARNING TO TALK TO PLANTS

MARTA ORRIOLS

AT NIGHT ALL BLOOD IS BLACK

DAVID DIOP

SPARK

NAOKI MATAYOSHI

TALES OF TRANSYLVANIA

MIKLOS BÁNFFY

ISLAND

SIRI RANVA HJELM JACOBSEN

CARMILLA

SHERIAN LE FANU

ARTURO'S ISLAND

ELSA MORANTE

ONE PART WOMAN

PERUMAL MURUGAN

WILL

JEROEN OLYSLAEGERS

TEMPTATION

JÁNOS SZÉKELY

BIRD COTTAGE

EVA MEIJER

WHEN WE CEASE TO UNDERSTAND THE WORLD

BENJAMIN LABUTUT

THE COLLECTED STORIES OF STEFAN ZWEIG

STEFAN ZWEIG